Flying and Falling

LYNDA TOMALIN

GlitterInk PRESS

CHAPTER 1

Hollie

I'M FLYING.

It's a moment of perfection, of weightlessness, of freedom.

Then a slight bump, a readjustment as Milo's hooves hit the ground and we move together away from the jump.

I steady him, then canter smoothly around the arena, his hooves making rhythmic thuds against the sandy surface. Easing him down to a walk, I stroke his muscled sweat-damp neck, sweeping his mane to one side to scratch at his favourite spot. The horse shakes his head, stretching out his neck as I give him rein.

Beth climbs down from the fence surrounding the arena, awkward with her six-month-old baby, Thea, secured to her front in a carrier.

"Good work. You guys are looking great." She strokes Milo's nose as he reaches over to say hello to the baby. "Don't over-do the jumping this week; let yourselves have a break, but keep up the fitness. Take him out for a hack or something." She scratches behind his ears. "But you'd better hurry or you'll be late for school."

Thea fusses for a second, then lets out a full-bodied wail.

Beth sighs. "Here we go again."

I sigh too. The freedom, strength and power jumping gives me drain away, leaving me with the usual heavy feeling that now follows me everywhere. I slide off Milo, patting his neck and rubbing his nose when he turns to snuffle me.

"Thanks, Beth," I call after her. "I'll see you later."

The March sun is beating down and it's only 7:30 in the morning. I cool Milo down, then slide the saddle from the big horse's back and hose the sweat off him, getting soaked by the spray every time he shakes his head or swishes his tail.

I try to enjoy this time, because I'll have to spend the next six hours trapped in stuffy classrooms, surrounded by people that, on the whole, I hate being around. Of course, there are one or two exceptions, but the vast majority of students at my school are definitely not my kind of people. I'd much rather be here with Beth and Milo and the other horses.

Milo is Beth's horse - all of them are - but I like to pretend he's mine. He's a gorgeous dark bay: a chocolate-brown coat with a slight reddish tint, and a black mane, tail and legs. A splash of white across his head is the only marking on him. He's not even sixteen hands high, so not big for a competitive showjumper, but his size suits me fine.

Not that he's a particularly competitive showjumper with me on his back. Before Beth got pregnant with Thea, they were ranked second in the area circuit. But then Thea happened, and Beth stopped riding in the fall-out of whatever happened with the baby's father.

I don't know the details. I mean, why would Beth share her personal life with the random girl she was effectively guilt-tripped into giving a job to? But I have heard she gave him the boot before anyone knew she was pregnant. Maybe *she* didn't even know. Either way, he's long gone.

When I needed a job, or anything to get me out of the house in the wake of the diagnosis, Mum arranged for me to start working for Beth. I know what I'm doing around horses, but I gave up riding my own horse last year.

It's a good job. I didn't realise how much I'd missed being around the animals until I started coming here.

As well as giving me something to do with my time, it checks off some other treatment requirements, including being outside, getting some sunshine and keeping active. And riding sure as hell beats running, though I still have to do that at least a couple of times a week.

"I promise I'd much rather be here with you," I murmur to Milo as I scrape the excess water away and dry him off. He nickers and lips at my sleeve. I rest my head against his neck and my hand finds his favourite spot for scratches under his mane.

An engine flares to life and I glance up. There's a dark green car rolling up the driveway. I've never seen it before. I definitely didn't see it when I arrived, so it must have been parked in the garage. Who could it belong to? Not that it's any of my business.

"C'mon Milo," I say, untying his lead rope. I'm going to be very late for school if I don't hurry up. He follows me towards the paddock. As soon as I unclip the rope he trots away, joining the few horses Beth has left.

Before Thea, she had a whole string of them, mostly belonging to other people who paid her to ride for them. It sounds like a dream job, except for living up to the crazy high expectations of the owners.

I grab my bag from the car and slip in the side door of Beth's house, through the laundry and into the downstairs bathroom. It's suddenly cool inside the old farmhouse, and I take a moment to savour it before stripping my horsey clothes off to step into the barely warm shower. I wash away the arena grime and sweat and try not to think about the day ahead.

The actual schoolwork is fine; it's the people, and having to bear the weight of their heavy expectations, that fills me with dread.

But there's nothing I can do about it. It must be done.

I shut off the shower, dry quickly and pull on school clothes. Tying my hair into a loose braid finishes it off. I check my phone for the time, and curse. I really am going to be late.

I'm most definitely not flying anymore.

CHAPTER 2

Jonathan

BREATHE.

Breathe.

In and out.

That's it.

That's all I have to do.

Breathe, breathe, breathe.

I'm sitting in my car at the far end of the carpark staring at the buildings in front of me.

My new school.

Students are standing around in groups, and most are beginning to wander towards the classrooms. Girls are tossing their hair, guys are checking out the girls as they toss their hair. There's laughing. A lot of it. And more than one couple making out. God, it all looks so simple – like my life was only a few months ago.

I've been sitting here for at least half an hour. I slipped out of my aunt's house as soon as I could this morning. I didn't need the inquisition I know she had lined up for me, or the perplexed looks or over-the-top kindness while she tries to figure out why I gave up my life to move here and shovel horse shit for her.

I study the crowds, the buildings, taking in my new surroundings. My hands clench the steering wheel. I only realise when my knuckles start to ache.

Five minutes to the bell.

There are only a few stragglers in the carpark now and I need to find the office, sign in, get my timetable, then start finding my classes.

Another deep breath.

Another.

I grab my backpack, slide out of the car and slam the door behind me.

Staring down the building, I stride across the carpark. A silver car comes hurtling down the row and I stumble as I throw myself out of the way. My palm hits the concrete and heat flares across my skin.

The hatchback is stopped now, beside where I'm sprawled on the ground. I climb to my feet and wince as I swipe my grazed palm across the denim of my jeans.

"What the bloody hell!" I slam my uninjured hand on the bonnet of the car and turn my angry glare on the driver.

The girl sits frozen for a second, hands grasping the steering wheel. The moment our eyes meet she leaps into action, jumping out of the car and rushing towards me.

"Oh my God. Are you okay?" She looks up at me and she must see anger in my expression, and frustration.

She stops. Takes a breath.

"I'm so sorry," she says, her voice quieter, less panicked. "I didn't see you. Are you okay?"

I study her for a moment, my feelings bubbling below the

surface. I take in the loose braid, wisps already escaping and falling around her face, her pink t-shirt and denim shorts, and take a breath myself.

"I'm fine," I mumble, no longer able to look at her, shame washing over me. Once upon a time I'd have laughed that off, made a joke and probably flirted with this girl. I definitely wouldn't have lost my shit. "I'm sorry," I say. "I shouldn't have walked out in front of you."

"I was late, going too fast." She raises a hand towards me as if to touch my arm and I notice her trembling.

"It wasn't your fault. I need to go. Don't worry about it." I slide away from her, stride across the carpark and disappear into the sea of students congregating outside classrooms.

CHAPTER 3

Hollie

WHY DO mornings drag so badly? Without fail?

The time I spent with Milo flew by, but now, sitting in class, the time is crawling.

I make a half-hearted attempt at taking notes, hand in last night's homework, follow along with whatever the teachers are rambling on about.

I don't hate school, but it's not exactly riveting stuff. I tolerate it and I get good marks because I have to.

Because it's expected of me.

Because despite the job at Beth's being part of the recovery plan, and Mum being fairly understanding about everything, she'll still stop me spending all my free time at Beth's if I don't keep my marks up. And that's something I'd rather not consider. I've given up riding once before and I can't contemplate doing it again.

I sit at the lunch table across from Kaitlin, picking at my food. She's gushing about the date she went on last night with Connor, about the way his hair falls and the way his smile "makes her all fizzy inside".

I guess you had to be there.

I wasn't there. Obviously.

Kaitlin tried to make me go and suggested I bring Dan, as if I'd suddenly admit that we were madly in love and yes please, could we double-date with her and Connor?

That's never going to happen.

I love Kaitlin. She's been my best friend for as long as I can remember. But over the past few months I've struggled to find anything we have in common. She talks about dating and Connor and parties and makeup, all conversations to which I have absolutely nothing to add. It's hard to be excited about those things when you'd rather not leave the house.

I have actually spent plenty of time with Dan, doing things Kaitlin would class as dates. But I can't tell her that. First of all, they definitely weren't dates, and second, this is Daniel we're talking about.

Daniel with the wild sandy curls falling like a golden halo around his head. Daniel with the infectious grin. Daniel who yeah, maybe at one time I did want to date.

Unfortunately, Kaitlin knows about the crush I once had on him – but she doesn't know all the stuff that came afterwards. All the stuff that's made him far too important a part of my life to risk losing him because of a frivolous relationship gone bad.

Not that he's interested in dating me, so the point is moot.

But I can't explain to Kaitlin what Dan means to me. Not without telling her everything, and that story's too heavy to contemplate telling anyone.

"You and Danny should have come," she begins, and I try desperately not to roll my eyes. Here we go.

I shrug and quell a snort.

"Kait …" I trail off as a mop of dark hair over Kaitlin's shoulder catches my eye.

The guy from this morning. The one I almost ran over with my car.

I feel my cheeks heat, and at the same time my stomach bottoms out from recalling the horror when I thought I'd hit him. His face flashes through my memory and I try to shake off the pure venom in his gaze as he looked down at me.

He stalks across the courtyard with his backpack slung over one shoulder. He's all long sweeping motion, sun highlighting touches of gold in his dark hair. It's a little too long and hangs in his face, obscuring his eyes, but it looks like there was an actual style there in the not-too-distant past.

His jeans are the perfect type – swagger and style but not so much that he looks pretentious – and his dark green t-shirt accentuates the colour of his hair and the tan on his arms.

He's glancing around as he walks and I feel myself shrinking, hoping he won't see me. He's heading in our direction but his gaze flicks over me and everyone else. He saunters on by to the stone retaining wall that edges the garden, and settles himself in the shade of a tree, alone.

A hand waves in front of my face.

"Earth to Hollie!"

I switch my attention back to my friend. She's staring at me, eyebrows raised.

"Sorry. What did you say?"

"I was giving you plenty of evidence for why you and Danny are already more than friends and should make it official already!" She glances over her shoulder to see what caught my notice. "But … who is that?"

He's pulled headphones out and slid them over his ears.

With one foot propped up on the wall, he starts scribbling furiously in a battered notebook.

"I don't know," I reply. "I saw him this morning, but I've never seen him before that."

She watches him for a moment. "I wouldn't mind seeing a bit more of him," she giggles.

"Oh, settle, girl." I whack her on the arm and grin. It's a glimpse of our friendship from the past, and I use the feeling to refocus our conversation, steering Kaitlin away from Dan and the new guy.

But I can't help my eyes sliding over to watch the dark-haired guy who barely glances up from his notebook for the rest of lunch. He doesn't eat a thing.

I sip my drink and grimace. The Coke is warm and mostly flat already. Apparently only alcoholic drinks are kept in the fridge at this party, despite over half of the attendees being under eighteen. Holding the drink is something to do with my hands though, so I don't ditch it.

Kaitlin's here somewhere, probably tucked away in a corner with Connor. I haven't seen them for what feels like hours, but it's more likely less than one.

A Friday night party with people from school is not my scene at all and I've got an early training session tomorrow, but I came to keep my best friend happy. There was no way out of it without upsetting Kaitlin, and as disconnected as we are these days, I still hate upsetting her.

I hate upsetting anyone.

I compromised and promised to pick her and Connor up,

but I'd be leaving early. She reluctantly agreed but said there was no way I was allowed to leave before 10:30.

Like I said, I hate upsetting people, especially Kaitlin. I'd almost walk through hot coals for her. Well, I'd seriously contemplate it.

Her face when I agreed to come was totally worth it. Plus, I keep being told, over and over again, that socialising and pushing myself out of my comfort zone is an excellent part of my therapy.

I'm leaning against a wall in a shadowy corner, scanning the crowd. I've chatted to a few people, danced with Kaitlin when she forced me to, and now I'm counting down the minutes until I can leave.

I actually don't mind dancing, and with Kaitlin it's always fun – if I can let my guard down enough. It's letting the guard down that's hard work.

Dan's here somewhere, too. I saw him earlier and he picked me up and spun me around, to the disgust of the latest girl whose eye he's caught. The thing about Dan, though, is that while I've seen him flirt like an absolute master and the girls line up for him, he hasn't shown any interest in a relationship since Year Ten. He had a girlfriend for a while, and they were the "it" couple of our year group until her family moved away.

Dan has this completely carefree attitude towards every-thing, which is one of the reasons I like being around him so much. He makes it all easy.

But I'm hesitant about spending too much time around him tonight. Kaitlin's words from yesterday are still rattling around in my head, about how we behave like we're more than friends already. Is that what everyone thinks?

It's not the first time Kaitlin's got carried away in her

enthusiasm for something, but it makes me feel awkward around him – which is ridiculous, because I know he feels the same way I do. We're friends. That's all we'll ever be and that's exactly how we both want it.

I take another sip of my drink. Nope, I can't do it anymore. I head for the kitchen and tip the remainder down the sink, tossing the cup into the bin. The clock on the kitchen wall reads 10:30.

I breathe a sigh of relief and weave my way back through the mass of bodies grinding to some vaguely familiar hip-hop beat.

I'm looking for Kaitlin. It's probably a wasted effort. She's staying with the girls from the soccer team tonight, and who knows where Connor is staying, but he's a big boy and doesn't need me to ferry him home.

I pull out my phone and slide my fingers across the screen, sending a quick text to Kaitlin letting her know I'm leaving. I'll text her again when I'm home so she doesn't worry. We're in completely different places most of the time, but she always cares.

I slip out of the house without being noticed and set off towards my car. It's a nice night and the stars are out. There's a gentle breeze, welcome after the searing temperature of the summer days and the oppressive, smothering heat inside the party.

It's a strange feeling being out in the peaceful night, with the thumping vibrations of the party behind me. It's like I'm here, but not really. Like I'm slightly disconnected from the real world. It's a feeling I'm used to, but for once it doesn't make me sad.

I take a deep breath of the cool air and grip the car keys

tightly in my fist. We were lucky to find a park close to the house, so I don't have to walk too far alone.

I'm approaching my car when I hear a thump and someone curses violently, shattering the quiet night. It's a male voice, filled with frustration and anger.

I hesitate, trying to gauge which direction it came from and if I should be worried about them, or myself.

Hyperaware, I skirt around the front bumper of my car. Adrenaline is shooting through me. That guy could be anyone, have any kind of intentions. Granted, if he was out here stalking me he probably wouldn't have given himself away by swearing so loudly.

There's a flash of movement and I see him. He's sitting on the asphalt, leaning against the driver's side door of the car parked in front of mine. It's some kind of retro cool car, in a dark moody colour. I couldn't tell you what kind it is though; they're not really my specialty. Give me horse colours, breeds and markings any day.

The movement that caught my eye was the guy lifting his hand to bury it in his dark hair.

I pause. There's something about him. He's looking utterly dejected while literally sitting in the gutter.

Then it clicks.

It's the new guy from school. The one I almost ran over.

"Um, hi," I say.

I can't leave him sitting there in the street.

He jumps at my voice and looks up. His face is defensive but exhausted, his eyes shadowy in the streetlight's glow, his hair tousled and falling into his face from when he jerked his hand free. He scrambles to stand, knocking his elbow on the car door and swearing again.

"Sorry," he mutters. "Uh, hi." He shifts uneasily, unable to meet my eyes. This whole exchange is awkward, but I don't know how to get out of it. I don't know what to do next.

"Are you okay?"

He fiddles with the keys in his hand.

"Ah yeah. Um, things are great." He still hasn't looked up. I'm not sure he's realised that I'm the girl who almost ran him down.

"I've not actually come across someone sitting in the street before, literally in the gutter, but I imagine something must be not great for you to be here like this."

He shifts again, shoving a hand into his pocket. I watch the movement and study him. He's pretty tall, likely even taller than Dan. I take in the dark hair – still rumpled – then what I can see of his face in the shadows. It's all angles and planes like the rest of him. I remember the cat-like way he stalked across the court at school. His eyes are too shadowed to see much of them, but I'm pretty sure he still hasn't looked at me properly.

"I dropped my keys," he mutters finally. "I hit my head picking them up, needed to sit for a bit."

"Are you driving home?"

"No." One word, but the snarl in it is off the scale.

"Do you have a ride?" I ask. Why am I even bothering?

"What's with the twenty questions?" he snaps, finally raising his head to look at me. Recognition flickers across his features, but it doesn't make them any friendlier.

"I'm trying to figure out if you're actually okay, because you don't look it, and if you need me to drive you somewhere."

He studies me silently and I shift my weight under his gaze, fidgeting with my keys.

"I've seen the way you drive," he says, and I flinch. "I don't need any fucking help. Everything's just fucking fine." His voice is rising and I take a step back. I can feel heat creeping up my neck, spreading into my face and burning behind my eyes.

"All right." I raise my hands in placatory gesture. Or maybe it's a protective move. "I was only trying to help."

I go to turn away but his voice stops me. It's quiet, but his words carry easily on the gentle breeze. The sound of the party is a distant thrum.

"I know. I'm sorry. Thanks."

I turn back to him and the aggression has fallen away. He's back to being the dejected guy I found sitting in the gutter. He lets out a deep, earth-shuddering sigh, dropping his head.

I drop my voice too.

"Seriously though," I say, "do you have a way to get home?"

He glances up, and I find myself staring into his eyes. It's impossible to see what colour they are.

Gently, at odds with how he was behaving a moment ago, he shakes his head. "I was supposed to drive, but I stupidly drank. The only person I could call has a baby and needs all the sleep she can get. So looks like I'm sleeping here."

"You can't catch a ride with the people you came with?"

"I didn't come with anyone. I don't know anyone here. I've only been here two days." There's a slight edge in his voice again.

I know he's new around here, but surely he must have come with someone. I'm sure I saw him inside with a bunch of guys from school, the rowdy ones who were at school only because they were forced to by their parents. The ones who sit in the back of classrooms making crass jokes and disrupting everyone. How did he even hear about the party if he doesn't know anyone?

"Some people were talking about tonight in Chemistry. I needed to get away from that baby I mentioned."

I nod, then wave towards my basic little hatchback.

"It's nothing compared to your machine, but I can give you a ride."

"Are you kidding me? You don't know me. You shouldn't go around inviting strange guys into your car! I mean, do you even know my name?" His voice is rising again, but not in anger this time.

I realise I'm being lectured. And what makes it worse is he is right about all of it. I hate going anywhere alone, especially at night, and to pick up a random stranger and let him in my car is crazy.

But standing here in the fuzzy orange glow from the streetlights, this boy doesn't seem threatening. Maybe it's because of how I found him, broken in the gutter. But even when he was angry, he wasn't scary.

"No. I don't know your name. And I wouldn't normally give a random stranger a ride, but I know you go to our school and I'm going to text my friend right now and tell him I'm driving you home, so he'll know where to come looking for me if I disappear." I cross my arms and raise an eyebrow in defiance, waiting for him to challenge me.

Instead, he laughs. It's like it releases something in him. He's not angry anymore and he's lost that dejected air. A smile crosses his face and there's a spark in his eyes.

"Okay, fair. But where I live is kind of out of the way, so don't worry about it. I know all about the consequences of poor decision making." There's a flicker in his face and the smile fades for a second.

"Out of curiosity's sake, where do you live?" I'm not ready to give up yet. I don't know why, but the idea of leaving him here alone to sleep in his car is heartbreakingly sad.

"Um, it's in that horsey area just north of town." He waves a hand in what I can only assume is the right direction. Navigation is not one of my strong suits.

"Oh." I'm surprised for a moment. "So right by me, then."

He looks at me, startled. "Really? Or are you trying to get me in your car? Should I be worried for my safety?" His mouth twitches a little and I smile, feeling a strange brush of heat across my cheeks. It's a nice feeling to be able to make someone smile.

"No. Seriously. I also live in that horsey area just north of town."

A silence extends between us. He watches me carefully and under his scrutiny I begin to fidget. I don't like people looking at me this closely. I fiddle with my keys, shift my weight from foot to foot and glance anywhere but directly at him. I'm about to open my mouth to tell him not to bother when he speaks first.

"You're not going to let this go, are you?"

I shake my head despite the fact that I was indeed going to let it go. "You live right by me, so there's no point sleeping in your car."

"Not much sleeping gets done in there, to be honest," he says, looking relieved at being rescued from that eventuality.

I smirk at him. I'm pretty sure he didn't mean for it to sound the way it did, but I'm constantly surrounded by teenagers whose minds live in the gutter.

"I – I didn't mean it like that," he says, noticing my look and stumbling over his words. "I mean, it's not very comfortable."

"Sure you didn't mean it like that," I say, and on the inside I'm surprised. Am I teasing him? Am I *flirting* with him? Who even am I anymore? "So you coming, then?" I indicate my car.

"Yes ma'am," he says, moving towards my car.

"Good God, don't ever call me that again."

He grins at me over the roof as I unlock the doors from my side. "All right, but only if you tell me what I can call you."

I slide into the driver's seat and start the ignition. There's a second of silence before the interior of the car is filled with beat-driven but exceedingly twangy country music. Very, very loud music. I flinch, and he quickly turns the volume down.

"My bad," I say, mentally banging my head against the window. Kaitlin had control of the stereo on the drive over and I forgot about our intense singalong. Country music isn't big around here and it's a guilty pleasure for both of us.

"So," he says, seemingly unaffected by the music choice, "what was it that I should be calling you?"

"Hollie." I smile over at him, and he holds out a hand.

"Nice to meet you. I'm Jonathan."

CHAPTER 4

Jonathan

"UP HERE ON THE LEFT," I say, and Hollie slows the car.

I've guided her through the quiet night streets. I tried other conversation too, but it was stilted, so I gave up and we sat in silence. It wasn't exactly uncomfortable though, and I didn't mind the quiet as she manoeuvred the little car. Her music was playing softly in the background and I smiled at the thought of her face when she'd started the car and it blasted through the speakers.

"You live here?" she asks, glancing over at me, skepticism all over her face and in her voice.

"Uh, yeah," I say. "It's my aunt's place. Is that an issue?" I'm confused as hell by her tone. But she doesn't answer, simply edges around potholes and bumps in the driveway with ease, which is surprising because I still haven't managed to make it without hitting at least three. She pulls the car to a stop under the huge tree by the barn and unlatches her seatbelt.

Still puzzled, I do the same. This girl is behaving super weird.

She studies me in the darkness for a moment, then pushes open her door and climbs out of the car.

Here I was thinking this was my place.

"You've been here before?" I ask stupidly, as I follow her towards the paddock fence. She leans against the railings and makes the clicking sound with her tongue that only horse people seem to be able to make.

"I'm here every day. I'm probably here more than I'm at school."

A huge shadow emerges out of the darkness and ambles towards us, and I suddenly realise that she's the girl Aunt Beth mentioned; the one who looks after the horses.

The shadow slides its nose over Hollie's shoulder and huffs into her hair while she reaches up to stroke its neck.

"Have you met him yet?" she asks, and I shake my head. I haven't made it to the horses yet.

"Jonathan, this is Milo," she says. The horse leans his head in my direction to sniff at my offered hand. I slide my knuckles down his velvet-smooth muzzle and smile slightly as he nibbles at me with his oversized, floppy lips.

"You ride here?" I ask her, but I already know the answer. I'm scratching Milo behind his ear, which he seems to appreciate very much.

"Yeah," she says. "Like I said, I pretty much live here, if I'm not at school."

"Or if you're not rescuing strangers from the gutter," I say.

She smiles. It turns out being around people is infinitely easier than being alone with my thoughts all day. I've spent less than half an hour with Hollie and I feel immeasurably lighter, like the bricks I've been carrying on my back the past few months are being held by someone else as well, even if only for a moment.

The other possibility is that the booze I laid into at the party has taken the load off me. I know from experience I'm going to badly regret that in the morning.

"You didn't know I'm staying here, then?" I ask, puzzled. Maybe Beth doesn't want people to know I'm here. She had mentioned Hollie to me, except of course I didn't know she was talking specifically about Hollie. And I wasn't exactly paying attention. I have a vague recollection of her telling me the girl who took care of the horses was my age, like she hoped we'd be friends. I almost told her I'm not five and don't need setting up on playdates to make friends, but I managed to squash the snark for a few minutes.

Hollie shakes her head. "I haven't seen Beth today, and yesterday it was only briefly. I was running late for school." She pauses, drops her gaze and shifts awkwardly from foot to foot. "I'm really sorry about what happened in the carpark."

I shrug, trying for nonchalance. "It wasn't your fault."

But she's shaking her head before I even finish speaking. "I was going way too fast. Like I said, running late."

This time I'm shaking my head. "How about instead of rehashing this over and over, you let me take the blame. I promise I'm well versed in it and can handle it." There's a hint of bitterness creeping into my voice and I try to push it down.

"How about," Hollie says, countering me, "we both accept and share fault for that incident and move on, never to speak of it again?"

"Deal," I say, and I even manage a smile. I'm lying through my teeth. The blame sits firmly between my shoulder blades, along with everything else.

"So what brings you here?" Hollie asks, leaning against the fence railings while the big horse snuffles her shoulder.

"Beth needed an extra set of hands," I say, holding mine up and waving them in front of my face. "Mine are as good as any, I suppose." I don't add that they're far more adept at making music than they are at manual labour.

Hollie pushes back from the fence and turns to face me again. Her expression is making me uncomfortable. "You gave up your life, moved away from your family and switched schools in the middle of term to help your aunt?"

I shrug, turning to the horse so I don't have to see her looking at me like I've done something amazing. I haven't. It's my escape, a purely selfish move. But I'm not telling some random girl this. I've already told her too much. I lean my head on the railings.

"It's not a big deal," I say quietly. "But I need some water, and some sleep, and I assume you need to get home."

She watches me for a moment. I can feel her eyes on me. "Yeah, I do need to go. I've got to be back here early to get everything done. I suppose I'll see you then."

I'm not sure if it's a question or not, and my uncertainty delays any kind of response. Before I can gather my wits she's turned away, crunching across the gravel back to her little hatchback.

"Thanks for the ride," I call, but I'm too late. She doesn't hear me.

I stay at the fence while she starts the car and pulls up the driveway, the gravel crunching beneath her tyres.

I drop my head to rest against the fence again. A pounding has already started in my temples and I'm not sure if it's from the alcohol or from hitting my head when I dropped my keys. I don't even know how it happened. I wasn't *that* drunk. Definitely too drunk to drive, but not drunk enough to be whacking my head against vehicles. I let out a sigh and hot air blows down my neck.

"Oi," I say, reaching up to push the horse's face away. What was his name again? Mouse? Milky? Milo?

"Milo?" I ask the horse, as if he's going to answer. I'm sure that's it, though. He's trying to eat my sleeve and I let him.

I don't know what I was thinking going to that stupid party. I've been at school for two days. I have a grand total of zero friends. I've never had to actively make friends either; there's always been Luke and we never had to try. I'm still completely undecided on the "should I make friends" question anyway. Is it worth it?

But a couple of guys were talking about the party behind me in class and then a girl with impressive blue streaks in her black hair joined their conversation and somehow I was right in the middle of the discussion.

Jake and Simon introduced themselves, inviting me along. They seemed like idiots – the kind of guys who think mean jokes at the expense of other people are funny – but my alternative was sitting at home with Beth, who looks at me with a weird expression of sadness mingled with hope that I might tell her what's going on in my head.

So I went, planning to hang out for a bit, maybe meet a couple of people and try not to stand out from the crowd, before heading home late enough to avoid Beth.

But my phone started going off with messages and phone calls, over and over.

My old life coming back to haunt me.

Jake offered me a beer, then Simon did, then the girl with the blue and black hair whose name I still can't recall.

It's easier to drown the memories; say yes and ignore the string of messages on my phone. Then I hit that stage of being drunk when you realise that you're drunk but weren't supposed to be and suddenly it's not that much fun anymore.

I made the mistake of pulling out my phone to check the time. A bunch of messages and missed calls filled the screen, and I made the even bigger mistake of reading them.

A stupid party with strangers is never going to take away what happened. A few beers aren't going to erase history, wipe clean what I did. So I took off, hoping to hide out in my car until morning when I'd be sober enough to drive. I'm a total asshole, but driving drunk is never going to happen.

Then Hollie emerged out of the darkness and brought me back to this place, which I guess now is home.

CHAPTER 5

Jonathan

THERE'S someone in the laundry room. I'm sure of it. Normally I wouldn't find it so concerning except I know for a fact that Aunt Beth is upstairs with the baby.

Thea.

I should stop calling her "the baby". I suppose she's a real person. It's a strange thing to contemplate after her being referred to as "the baby" for so long.

Anyway, I can hear Beth and Thea upstairs and I saw them with my own eyes moments ago as I staggered past, bleary-eyed. Beth was pacing the room with Thea crying against her shoulder.

So it definitely isn't Beth in the laundry.

Maybe I'm not fully awake yet.

I spoon instant coffee into a mug and switch on the jug. I miss real coffee already. After spending three months making fancy barista coffees for city dwellers and having full access to the machine at whim, switching back to instant has been tough.

I cross the room and push open the door that leads to the

laundry and downstairs bathroom, between the kitchen and side door.

I was right. There is someone in the laundry.

My brain takes a moment to catch up with the situation. Someone in a pair of jeans and the brightest pink socks I've ever seen is bending down, shoving a handful of clothes into the washing machine. I can't see her face. I'm assuming it's a she based on the pink socks and rather appealing curve of hips in jeans. It's an assholey assumption, and it would serve me right after everything if it was a guy.

But it's not.

The girl straightens, two blonde braids falling down her back, and turns. Hollie is standing there in my frickin' laundry, holding a washing basket full of what looks suspiciously like my clothes.

Oh my God. She's washed my clothes.

My hand flies to my back pocket. My empty back pocket. But wait: these weren't the jeans I was wearing last night. I left those on the bathroom floor when I stumbled inside and showered, hoping to sober myself up.

Unfortunately, it did the trick.

But *please* let her not have washed those clothes.

Hollie startles a little when she sees me. Her eyes flick down and quickly back up to my face. I realise I'm shirtless, but at least I put on pants. I think we're both a little relieved by that. Her cheeks flush red and her surprise slides into a small smile.

"Hi," she says, like it's totally normal that she's doing laundry in my new home.

"What the fuck are you doing in here?" The words are out of my mouth and hanging between us before I have a chance to think about them or register what is going on here.

Panic is sliding down my spine and settling over me.

Her mouth opens, but no words come out. She closes it and tries again. "Um, I was switching over the washing for Beth." She reaches out and presses some buttons on the machine, which bleeps into life.

"Do you routinely go through other people's washing? Or am I special?" The snark is off the scale this morning. I'm bloody hungover and the baby – sorry, Thea – was up half the night screaming and now this random girl I've met once is going through my clothes. Going through someone's washing crosses the damn line.

She stares at me, silent. I watch as she takes a deep breath. I see her chest rise, then fall as she lets the breath out long and slow.

"I'm only helping Beth," she says eventually. Her voice is quiet and somehow steady, even with a jackass shouting at her. Because we all know I'm a jackass. "I come by sometimes, between jobs outside, and hang out the washing or do the dishes. I didn't mean to offend you; I'm really only trying to help her."

With that, she shoves the basket at me, turns on her heel and heads out the side door, stamping roughly into her boots and striding across the lawn.

I remain standing in the doorway, frozen to the spot, clutching the washing basket. I'm not sure I know what the hell just happened.

As I move to put the basket down a voice calls out behind me and my insides curl in shame to know Beth probably saw the whole thing.

"Could you please hang that out for me?"

I turn to see Beth leaning against the kitchen bench. "Since you chased Hollie away and all. She really is trying to help. She thinks she owes me because I let her ride my horses. And I'm sorry," she continues, "I should have warned you that she sometimes helps out in here too."

I shake my head, waving away her apology. "I'll do the washing," I mutter, avoiding her gaze.

I glance down into the washing basket still clutched to my chest and realise that sitting on the top of the pile of wet washing is the shirt I wore last night. The shirt I dumped on the bathroom floor.

Damn her for being so damn helpful.

A cold chill runs down my back and I drop the basket with a thud to start rooting through it. I'm on my knees on the tile floor, flinging damp clothing in all directions.

My breath catches as I pull out dark-wash denim.

My eyes feel hot. It can't be gone. She can't have ruined it.

I slip my hand into the back pockets, expecting the feel of washed paper. But there's nothing there. Both pockets are completely empty. It's gone.

I slump onto the floor, leaning against the door. My head is pounding and my eyes are beyond hot. Now they're burning. I rub my hand across them, then slam it against the door frame.

"Woah, Jonathan!" Beth's voice is close and I crack open my eyes. "What's the matter? Is it Hollie?" She lays a hand on my arm, soft and gentle.

She's right there with me on the laundry floor. I drop my arm, letting her hand fall away.

My hand shakes and throbs, because hitting a wall isn't one of the greatest moves I've ever made. I'll add it to the list of stupid things I've done.

"No, it's not her." My voice is rough and spiky. "Don't worry."

I push myself upright, pushing away from Beth and her kindness. I don't want it. I don't deserve it.

And my reminder of exactly why I don't deserve it is gone.

Except it wasn't only a reminder of the pain I caused; it was also a reminder of the very best bits of my life. The life I used to have.

I turn away from Beth, avoiding eye contact at all costs, and glance out the window instead.

Something on the windowsill catches my eye. It's a handful of coins, a pen and a Polaroid photo. It's my photo.

I'm weak with relief.

It's there. It exists. It's not ruined.

Thank God for Hollie being a pocket checker.

I slowly drag myself up from the floor and reach for the picture. I study it for a moment. The edges are worn, the corners creased from constant handling. I'm going to ruin it myself if I'm not careful.

"Johnny." Beth rests her hand on my back. My mouth twitches into the tiniest smile at the use of my nickname. No one here calls me that. I feel like I left Johnny behind three months ago. "That's Luke?"

I can't speak yet, so I nod.

The picture was taken about six months ago from the top of a mountain bike track. Our faces are red with exertion, hair damp with sweat from our helmets. The view of pine forest stretches out behind us as we stand, facing the camera, arms around each other's shoulders. Luke's face is lit with triumph. Mine is exhausted. It was a massive climb and it took about three days for my legs to recover. Our smiles are wide and Luke's long black hair is falling into his eyes.

"His hair was always too long," I finally whisper. "I think he was afraid of hairdressers or something."

Beth laughs quietly. "Johnny, have you looked in a mirror lately?"

"What?" I finally turn to her, tearing my eyes from the picture gripped in my hand. Beth is still right there beside me, her hand now resting on my shoulder.

"Your hair. It's the longest I've ever seen it on you. Longer even than that time when you were ten and badly wanted heavy metal hair."

She reaches up and runs her fingers through it, smoothing it forward, and I realise she's right. It hangs down right past my eyes. I must look like a real ass. It probably goes well with my personality.

I don't say anything, but I can look at Beth again.

"Coffee?" she asks, taking a small step back, but not taking her hand away yet.

"Please."

"You know, Johnny … it's okay to talk about it. To talk about him. You must miss him, be upset about what happened." She pats my shoulder. "Talking has been known to help things, you know." She heads into the kitchen and I turn back to the window, looking out towards the barn.

Hollie's little silver car is under the big tree – the same place she parked it last night after she'd driven me home. Which she'd done because I was too stupid and too drunk to drive myself.

Then she came in here to help Beth, which is what I'm supposed to be here to do. The reality is, I've done nothing to help Beth, nothing to help anyone at all. I've made everything worse for everyone. Again.

I look back at the picture. It's my favourite ever taken of the two of us. I slip it into my pocket. Hollie must have seen it. I wonder if she thinks it's weird I carry a photo around with me. I pull the picture back out along with my phone and snap a shot of it, so at least I have a digital copy, before pushing them both back into my pocket.

"Coffee's up," Beth calls from the kitchen.

I slide into the chair at the kitchen table and she places a mug in front of me.

"Hey, Beth," I start, but my voice catches. I clear my throat and carry on. "Thanks for the offer, but I don't really want to talk about Luke."

"That's okay," she says, sitting down opposite me. "But I'm here if you want to, or if you want to talk about anything else. Don't get all caught up in that overly hairy head of yours."

I crack a smile at that one. "Rough night with Thea?" I ask. It's time for a subject change.

Beth groans and leans her head in her hands. "Sorry. We kept you up?"

I shake my head. "Not really. I heard her when I got in last night." I wasn't going to tell Beth that actually, I heard her a lot.

"Oh, I didn't hear your car, but maybe I heard you," she says, thinking for a moment. "Did you push it down the drive? Trying to sneak in?"

I laugh, then realise maybe it's not funny. Beth and I haven't really had a chance to lay down ground rules, with me arriving out of the blue and then avoiding her as much as possible ever since.

"I didn't know I had to sneak in." Then I remembered last night and Hollie picking me up out of the gutter to bring me home. "Uh, actually, Hollie drove me home."

Beth raises a single disapproving eyebrow at me, and I drop my eyes to study the rim of my coffee mug. Here comes the underage drinking lecture.

"So she drove you home and then you shouted at her? I know you've got a lot going on, but Johnny, that's really not okay."

Okay, so apparently the drinking isn't so much the issue as the whole being a crap human thing. Regardless, I shouldn't push the drinking issue too far. "I know, I know. I … I dunno, I was surprised to see her there. She told me last night she rode here, but I didn't expect to see her standing in the laundry. And the picture…" I trail off.

"Good thing I check pockets, right?" Beth pauses a moment and I realise I was blaming Hollie for doing my washing when it was Beth all along. She must have put it on earlier this morning.

"So where's your car? I can take you to pick it up later, but Thea needs to sleep first."

"It's okay. I suspect you could do with some more sleep too. I should go for a run or something anyway. I'll go get it."

She stares at me. She knows I'm not a runner. Mountain biking with Luke (after some persuasion) is all the exercise I've ever done. But she lets it go.

"After you've apologised to Hollie, right?" she says, and the eyebrow rises again.

"And hung out the washing." I drain the rest of my coffee and go to find a shirt.

CHAPTER 6

Jonathan

HOLLIE'S IN THE BARN.

I can see her boots behind a giant grey horse. I can hear her talking to it but can't actually see her.

Which means she probably has no idea I've been standing here trying to figure out what the hell to say to her. I go to take a step towards her but can't quite pull it off.

I was such a jerk. I shouldn't be allowed near people. I spent as long as possible sulking in my room after my talk with Beth and the drama of the laundry incident. Eventually I couldn't avoid reality anymore, and now it's time to confront my asshole tendencies.

Hollie moves towards the horse's head and I see her hand reach up and stroke its long face. Her face moves into view and she drops a kiss on the horse's nose.

I need to move. I need to say something. I'm standing here being creepy. A creepy jerk. Such a great impression for someone to have of me.

"Um, hi." I manage to croak the words out and her head jerks up. She sees me standing by the door and ducks under the horse's neck, towards me. She looks at me again – a cold, calculating look, judging me – then turns away to lift a saddle off the nearby rack and heave it over the giant's back. The horse turns to nuzzle at her and she gently pushes his face away.

I wait for a few more moments but she continues to ignore me, doing up buckles and adjusting straps, all the while murmuring to the horse.

I'm not sure what I was expecting, but I don't think it was this. It would be easier if she yelled at me. Maybe she knows that and is making it harder on purpose. Being ignored isn't something I'm used to.

I'm not used to apologies either. I didn't used to be a dick.

I force my feet forwards, taking a couple of steps in her direction. I open my mouth but no words come out. You'd think I'd have got better at doing this after recent events, but apparently not.

I clear my throat. My mouth is dry, my tongue thick and sandpapery.

"Hollie."

She doesn't look at me, so I step up beside her. Her cheeks are flushed. There's a smudge of dirt on one and loose strands of hair are falling softly about her face. She roughly pushes them back, which explains the smudge.

"Hollie," I say again. This time she glances at me, but looks quickly away. "Look, I'm … I'm sorry. I'm a jerk and I know you were helping Beth and … I'm sorry."

She's stopped fiddling with the saddle and is now stroking the horse's mane, angling her body away from me. I can see the tense set of her jaw as I stand awkwardly for a moment, waiting to see if she'll say something.

She doesn't, and I take a step backwards.

"I really am sorry. And thank you, for last night and for helping Beth." I'm turning to leave, my body engulfed by disappointment, regret, shame – I'm not even sure – when her voice catches me. It's only one word and it's barely audible, but it's her voice. I didn't know how much I needed her to speak to me until she did.

"Okay."

I pause in my retreat.

I'm supposed to be here to help Beth, and I know that so far I've made a pretty poor job of it.

Maybe I can win back that feeling I had last night driving with Hollie in the dark, and do something useful for my family – for someone, anyone. I take a deep breath and throw caution to the wind.

"So," I start, and Hollie slowly turns to look at me, an eyebrow raised, and I realise how much time she spends with Beth, because their expressions are identical. She knows I'm going to ask something and she's waiting to see how selfish my question will be.

I push on. "I'm here to help Beth. That's why I came. So can you let me know what needs doing out here?"

She's still studying me, that single eyebrow raised, not saying a word.

"If you want to, that is," I ramble. "I thought it might be easier for Beth if she didn't have to show me everything. But it's okay if you don't want to."

Considering how hard it was to get any words out a moment ago, I'm kind of shocked how quickly they're falling out of my mouth now. I'm not sure I could stop them if I tried. I fidget a moment longer under her steady gaze when I see her mouth twitch slightly on one side. I'm not sure if it's a smile or if she's fighting a frown.

"You might regret that," she says.

"I regret many things," I say, "but I don't think that getting you to hate me less is going to be one of them."

<hr>

God, she was right.

If I wasn't so damn angry with myself, I'd definitely regret my hasty move to leap into farm work this morning.

My head is still pounding. The coffee and painkillers I downed this morning are barely taking the edge off. The physical work around the barn and stable yard isn't helping.

Or maybe it is. Maybe it's a great way to vent my frustration with myself. Hard labour is about all I deserve at the moment. It feels more appropriate than spending my summer working in a posh café full of snobby city types. That job was almost fun.

I pause from shovelling the horse crap I was so excited to come and deal with, and catch my breath. I glance over to the paddock where Hollie is riding that massive grey horse.

Is it even a paddock? It must have a fancy horsey name. Wooden railings enclose it, and there's a matching wooden gate that is by far the best-quality gate around this place. The rest are basic steel and look like they're barely hanging on. The surface of the paddock or whatever it's called is dirt, or maybe sand. Colourful horse jumps are scattered about but there's still plenty of room for Hollie to ride around them. It's a big space.

I've been sneaking peeks over at her for the whole half hour I've been at work. She sits on the horse like she was born there. She moved through a series of gaits, changing direction in a succession of loops and zigzags around the paddock, before moving on to jumping. The horse, which I learned is a mare while Hollie was explaining what I needed to do, sweeps over the jump rails with room to spare. Hollie balances delicately on the horse's back, controlling her with signals I can't even see. It's amazing to watch.

After clearing the last jump Hollie slows the horse to a walk and leans down to pat her neck. They're headed in my direction and I realise she's going for the gate. I reach it before she does and swing it wide enough for them to pass through, sliding the latch into place again behind them.

"Thanks," Hollie murmurs as she passes by. She's breathing heavily, as is the horse, but the most remarkable thing is the look on Hollie's face.

Gone is the tense, cold look she gave me earlier. Instead, her face is split by a wide smile, her eyes sparkling and cheeks flushed with what I can only assume is happiness or adrenaline or something. Definitely not the same emotion that flushed them earlier in the barn when I made my apologies.

"That was ... wow," I say stupidly. "That was awesome to watch." Honestly, what this girl must think of me and my grasp on the English language and conversational skills, I don't even know, but it can't be good.

She laughs lightly. "Yeah. Alaska's a good girl. Aren't you?" She reaches down and ruffles the horse's mane. She looks up at me again. "Hey, could you hold her for a second while I grab Harley out?"

She slides off Alaska's back and my eyes linger on her denim-clad legs as she swings one clear over the horse's back and drops lightly to the ground. What the hell is wrong with me?

I pull my eyes away again and ask, "Harley?"

"Yeah, that little thing over there." She waves towards a little horse standing at the fence. "He needs some exercise but I don't have time to ride him and cool Alaska down properly, so he can tail behind us. Unless…" She trails off and slowly looks me up and down, from my stupid unsuitable shoes to my apparently too-long hair.

"Unless what?" I say, feeling a small stone of dread forming in the pit of my stomach. I do not like the look she has in her eye.

"Unless you want to help me with that?" She flashes me a coy little smile and the stone of dread grows heavier and does a somersault.

When I say nothing, she continues. "I thought you were here help?" She crosses her arms and raises that goddamn eyebrow again. I can't say I've ever thought anything in particular about an eyebrow raise, but God, it's the sexiest thing I think I've ever seen. She's staring me down and I get a grip on myself.

"But I can't ride."

She can't be serious. Doesn't she realise I'm a city boy? That the only callouses I've ever had are from fingering guitar strings? My hands right now are already blistering, my muscles aching. The only heavy lifting I'm used to is a tray of lattes for a bunch of arrogant businessmen.

She lets out a loud dramatic sigh. "Oh, shame. I thought you were trying to make up for being a jerk."

What the hell? I feel my blood start to rise and I try to keep a handle on it. She's got to be kidding, but the look on her face and the way she's holding her body makes me think she's really not.

"Are you serious? You want me to ride? That'll make you forgive me?" She's evil, I think. A sadist. Half of me wants to tell her to get stuffed and hate me, the other half says I'm already way too invested in getting this girl to forgive me.

"It would be super helpful," Hollie says, flashing me another coy smile, and I realise she *is* teasing me. She's mocking me. She knows how cheeky she's being, and despite me knowing this is a completely and utterly terrible idea, my stomach does that weird little flip again.

"I do this and you'll forgive me for being a jackass?"

"Well, I'll forgive you for being a jackass *this* time." She gives a little shrug and hands me Alaska's reins. "Hold her while I grab Harley. Who do you want to ride?"

I cannot believe she got me to do this.

I do not ride.

Well, I didn't. I suppose I do now. I readjust myself in the saddle, again, and take a few deep breaths.

"Okay," Hollie says, taking a few steps back from Harley's side. "Give him a little nudge with your legs to get him to move."

She's shown me how to hold the reins and how to sit my feet in the stirrups. Apparently I'm ready to go. I jiggle my legs a little, feeling like a complete fool, and to my surprise Harley takes a step forward.

I'm officially riding a horse. Who'd have thought?

"Great. Now the reins make him turn, but mostly he'll follow Alaska. We'll take it nice and slow."

She flashes me a grin over her shoulder as she gathers her reins and prepares to mount. She swings up onto Alaska's back with much more ease and grace than I used to get onto Harley, and I had the aid of a mounting block.

Hollie signals Alaska to start walking and they head towards the back corner of the yard, where the gate leads out to the paddocks. Awkwardly, I encourage Harley to follow.

Hollie was right. The little horse seems amiable enough and is quite happy to follow the big grey, regardless of my opinion on the matter. I watch Hollie and try to emulate her easy confidence on horseback.

She casually reaches down from her vantage point and unlatches the gate, swinging it wide for us to pass through, before manoeuvring Alaska around to close it behind us. Again, she does it all without any outward sign of controlling the horse.

"Ready to go?" She looks over at me, a strange look crossing her face when she catches me watching her. "What?" she says.

"You're really good at this horse thing, aren't you?

CHAPTER 7

Hollie

I FREEZE AT HIS WORDS. It's only for a second, but the question strikes me to my core, echoing through me.

Is he mocking me? I'm not sure, but I don't *think* so. He's sitting there watching me with this kind of surprised look on his face. I wish I hadn't asked him what it meant.

I feel heat creeping up my neck. I've dragged out the pause too long and he's casual as ever on Harley's back, still watching me far too closely.

"Uh, I dunno," I eventually manage to stammer. "I … I really love it. Horses make sense to me and they don't judge you and they aren't confusing and complicated. They are what they are and I understand them." I can't make eye contact anymore. I can't even look at Jonathan, so I fiddle with the reins instead, needlessly adjusting them.

Whyyyyyy did I have to say that? Why couldn't I have said, "Yeah, I suppose," and move on? Why did I have to be so freaking awkward?

"Well, you look pretty good to me." There's another pause,

and I definitely can't look at him this time. Did he mean it like it sounds?

I smooth Alaska's mane and give a little shrug.

He clears his throat. "So, um, where are we headed?"

I'm both grateful and a little envious of his ease with conversation. Simply getting words out of my mouth feels like I've run a marathon sometimes, and that's just random words. Getting the right words out seems almost impossible ninety-five percent of the time.

I point to the hill over my shoulder. "Up there."

His eyes follow where I've pointed and a flicker of emotion crosses his face – maybe nerves, but I can't really tell. It's smoothed over in a flash and his face is back to the relaxed confidence I wish I could emulate. He sends a little smile my way and nudges Harley forward.

"Well come on, then," he says, and I turn Alaska to follow.

The two horses pick their way along the track and I convince Jonathan to let Harley have his head to find his own footing, even though he's reluctant to release his grip on the reins.

Alaska walks calmly on a loose rein and I let the gentle sway of her gait roll through my body. A soft breeze sweeps down the hill and over me, and with each step I feel another weight being lifted from my chest.

The grass is long in this paddock and I watch as the green shifts and sways, buffeted by the wind. I focus on each of my senses, drawing on them to help calm myself.

I know this feeling that's been following me around this morning – the sickness in my stomach, my heart beating fast in my chest, a shakiness to my limbs, and the all-encompassing, overreaching feeling of dread – it's the feeling that something is going to go wrong.

This was never a situation I expected to find myself in, though no amount of preparation would have saved me anyway.

I'm floundering.

Do I talk to him? If I do, what about? Casual, inane things? Intelligent, probing questions about him? As if I'd be able to come up with something that falls into that category.

The biggest question churning around in my head is, should I still be mad at him for behaving like a total asshat this morning? Did I forgive too easily? Probably, but I also have this gut feeling that he's not really a jerk. That he's actually a nice guy. I don't know why, but I can't help feeling it was my fault. Except now there's a voice in my head demanding that I believe I wasn't in the wrong.

After a few false starts I manage to get words out.

"When we get to the hills," I start, as I guide Alaska to walk alongside Harley on the track, "you'll need to help him out a little and lean forward going up. Keep your heels down and lean back going down the hills."

I pause for a moment, watching him from the corner of my eye to see if I'm being way too basic for him. He's watching me, taking in the advice, and I notice his right hand is clenched around the pommel of the saddle, knuckles white.

"And if anything happens, grab his mane and don't let go."

He glances down at his hand, maybe noticing for the first time how tight he's been clutching the saddle.

"And the chances of something happening are what, exactly?"

"Pretty low," I assure him. "But they're horses. Don't shout at me again, hold on, and you should be fine."

The words are out and sitting in front of me, hanging in the air. What was I thinking bringing up the shouting again?

The dread spirals and swirls in my belly. I think I might be sick.

The issue is, I wasn't thinking. It's not like the scene in the laundry this morning is something I want to remember (despite it constantly replaying in my mind), and I definitely don't want to give him anything else to shout at me about.

I gently urge Alaska to lengthen her stride and pull ahead of Harley so Jonathan can't see my face – which I know is burning again – and I can't see his, which is probably filled with fury.

After he laid into me and I fled outside, I fought it hard, but I couldn't stop the tears. There were only a few, but they still came. I hate being shouted at. I hate conflict. I hate being in the wrong. I'd rather be ignored.

I know that helping Beth around the house is outside my job description. I'm there to ride the horses and look after them. But some evenings as I was getting ready to leave I'd notice the washing still on the line as darkness was creeping in, so I'd bring it inside. Some mornings I'd go into the kitchen to check if Beth wanted me to do anything specific that day and I'd notice dishes piled in the sink, or overflowing laundry baskets. I'd hear my mother's voice in my head and I'd start helping.

I know Beth's been doing it pretty tough, especially since the guy she had running the farm was injured and can't work anymore.

She always insists my extra work isn't necessary, but she

seems to appreciate it and she's never had any issue with me being in the house. She invites me in regularly, for coffee or occasionally dinner. I use the bathroom all the time. Neither of us seems to think it's a big deal. Apparently Jonathan does.

Thankfully I managed to quell the tears before he came out to the barn, though there was no doubt my face was red and blotchy. He apologised, asked for my help, and, I noticed as I left the arena, he'd hung out the washing.

I let out a long, slow breath. The pressure in my chest is back, pulling me down. A wave of sadness crashes over me as I realise the place I felt most comfortable and most welcome probably won't be the same now Jonathan is living there.

"Oof." Jonathan grunts and a moment later bounces up beside me after apparently urging Harley into a trot. Pulling up beside Alaska, the smaller horse is happy to return to a walk. I scratch Alaska in her favourite spot under her mane and avoid looking at the boy next to me.

"Look, I really am sorry about that." He sounds sincere, like he did earlier when he apologised. I don't know why my stupid brain brought it up again.

"I know. I'm sorry, I shouldn't have said that."

"No, it's okay. I've got a raging hangover and I really wasn't expecting to find anyone in the laundry this morning, let alone you. I had a moment. I shouldn't have yelled at you, and I promise it's not something I intend to do again. Cross my heart."

He looks so contrite, like a puppy who's been scolded, and I smile at the imagery. A hopeful little smile appears on his face.

"Raging hangover, you say? You know the best cure for that, right?"

"A lot of coffee and a lot of sleep?" he says, hopefully.

"No," I scoff. "Horse riding, obviously."

"Yeah, well, the fresh air might be good for it, but my ass disagrees with this whole situation."

A laugh bubbles up from nowhere. It's a good feeling, like the feelings I get in glimpses when I'm with Dan, or when I'm flying over a jump, balanced perfectly on a horse's back. I wish it was a feeling that came a little easier.

Jonathan's smile widens into a grin like he's won a prize, and I smile back, a strange buzzing settling in my stomach.

"You know," he says, as he gazes around the hillside, "I spent a bit of time up here when I was a kid. I always remember everything being a whole lot bigger."

"Well, you're bigger now."

"That's true," he nods. "And I bet this hill would be much harder work if I wasn't sitting on a horse. I remember climbing it and thinking it was a mountain."

"Yeah, Harley is doing a little more work than you."

Conversation is suddenly becoming easier again, and I almost feel like I used to, back before every word, every action, every thought became like a brick weighing me down. I push the thought away.

This is not the time to remember.

"Is it okay if I use the bathroom for a bit?"

Jonathan looks at me sideways as he latches the gate and we start back across the yard.

We rode for an hour, a gentle stroll through the hills, with conversation flowing easily. When we got back, Jonathan helped me unsaddle both horses and put them away in their paddock.

"Do you usually ask?" he says, a thoughtful expression on his face.

"Well … no. Beth doesn't mind. But it's not only Beth here now."

He smiles a little. "Thanks for your consideration, but you're good. Now I know about it I shouldn't have any more early-morning shocks."

"Promise I'll try to keep early morning shocking to a minimum. Can you put that away for me?" I toss the lead rope at him, which he catches easily, and turn towards my car to grab my bag.

Jonathan falls into step beside me as we make our way towards the house. He eyes the bag tossed over my shoulder. "Geez, I didn't say you could move in!" He's already starting to move stiffly. He's going to hurt later.

"Ha. No." I try to brush off the teasing, not letting my brain turn it into something it isn't, making me believe he doesn't want me here. The sensible part of my brain thankfully takes control. "I have somewhere to be and it's faster to get ready here than go home."

"Fair point." We take a few steps in comfortable silence. "So, how long do you reckon it's going to take me to walk to my car?"

This brings me up short. "You're going to walk to your car?"

"Well, maybe I'll run." He shrugs.

"It's a twenty-minute drive and you've been on a horse for an hour."

He looks thoughtful, and a little pained. "I hadn't factored in the horse bit. And shit, is it really twenty minutes? It did not feel like it last night." He sighs and ruffles a hand through his hair. It's a little sweaty around the edges from the riding helmet and it stays sticking up in random patches. The unusual buzzing in my tummy swoops like I'm on a rollercoaster, then resumes.

"It's not too far out of my way. Let me get ready and I'll drive you back."

"Seriously?" He almost wilts with relief.

"Yes," I say. "Conveniently, I am once again heading in that direction anyway."

"Thank you so much," he says in a rush. "Beth and Thea had a crappy night so I didn't want to ask her. Figured the walk would be a good penance for being an idiot."

"Maybe, but regardless, I will save you from your penance. Give me ten minutes."

CHAPTER 8
Jonathan

THE DOOR CREAKS open behind me and Hollie steps onto the deck, gently latching the door behind her.

"You ready to go?"

I nod and stand from where I've perched on the top step. I changed out of the dusty clothes I was wearing while working – if you can call it working – and pulled on a pair of shorts and a t-shirt, then waited for Hollie, fiddling with my phone and ignoring the messages that needed a reply.

I almost trip down the steps when I catch sight of her. She's worked some strange girl magic in those ten minutes and is almost completely transformed.

Gone are the dirt-smeared jeans and worn grey t-shirt with holes in the shoulder she was wearing earlier. Now she's standing in front of me in a black dress with tiny pink flowers all over it. A low V-neck shows off a hint of cleavage, though I don't let my eyes linger. The skirt ends slightly above her knees and swishes as she walks.

Her hair, released from its braids, falls over one shoulder in a blonde wave. She's put on makeup, her lips now a glossy pink, and quite honestly she looks like a total babe.

I mean, she's always pretty. I noticed it that first day in the parking lot when she almost ran me over. Even though we were both shocked, I could see she was gorgeous. You'd have to be completely oblivious not to. But I've also only ever seen her dressed casually.

Even last night at the party she wasn't dressed like this. I think she was in jeans and a blue tank top, though I don't have a particularly clear recollection. There's definitely one vivid memory of denim-clad legs working the clutch in her car.

I remember it because I was surprised she was driving a manual transmission. Not that I think she can't drive a manual because she's a girl. It's just that not many people do it anymore, and her little hatchback looks like an easy-to-drive auto.

Hollie's heels click along the deck and down the steps, crunching as she hits the gravel driveway, where she wobbles slightly before adjusting to the uneven surface. I realise I'm still standing dumbly on the steps and scurry to catch up to her.

"Got a hot date?" I ask, like a complete moron.

She looks at me over the roof of her car, rolls her eyes skyward and slides out of sight into the driver's seat. She shoves her bag into the backseat.

I open the door to climb in. "He's a lucky guy," I say. "Or she's a lucky girl."

"Oh, shut up." She shakes her head, but I think there's a hint of a smile touching her lips. She starts the engine, pumping the clutch a few times. "Oh, these stupid shoes." Reaching down, she fiddles with the ankle straps, slips the sandals off and tosses them over to me.

"Hold these for me; they're impossible to drive in."

"Can't say I've ever tried," I say with a laugh, eyeing the strappy contraptions. "But seriously, you look great."

"Uh, sure, thanks." Hollie's face turns a glorious shade of pink and I grin, but for once I'm not completely stupid and I do it facing away from her.

"Again, thank you for this."

"Yeah, sure," she says. "As if this wasn't your plan all along."

"What … what do you mean?"

She looks over at me. "As if you weren't being super helpful and all nice so I'd give you a ride."

That stops me in my tracks. My brain rakes over everything that's happened this morning. I haven't done it intentionally but I can see how it might look that way.

I open my mouth to protest, to assure her that isn't the case. She's smiling and I realise she might be mocking me.

"I…" I begin, but am cut off by a pounding drumbeat. Hollie jerks a little in fright.

"Sorry," I say, sliding my phone from my pocket. I look at the screen, reject the call and turn it face-down against my leg.

"You can answer it," Hollie says. "I'll try not to listen."

"Nah. It's not someone I need to talk to right now."

And it's not. It's really, really not.

My chest went tight at the glimpse I got of the caller ID. Snakes are curling in the pit of my stomach. I'm clenching my phone, pressing it into my leg like I was grasping the saddle earlier when I was riding Harley. I look out the window, searching desperately for something to hold onto, something to keep me here in this moment. My breath is shaking.

I should have known this would happen, that the calls

would start. You can't disappear one day and not have people wonder where you are.

Somehow though, I'm still surprised.

Then my phone rings again.

The sound of that drum beat cuts to my soul. I should change this stupid ringtone. But I've tried that before and couldn't go through with it. Besides, it's not just a stupid ringtone.

Hollie doesn't startle this time, but I feel her glance over at me then continue driving, focussing on the road ahead of us.

I reject the call again, this time silencing the ringer. It vibrates almost immediately in my hand.

The tightness in my chest turns to burning. The feeling is back, like anger but also not like anger. It roars through my head, blurring my vision. I toss my phone onto the console of Hollie's car and push myself back into the passenger seat in an attempt to ground myself.

My eyes fall to her hand resting on the gearstick. She's tapping her index finger against the knob, then her arm flexes as she smoothly changes up a gear. She hasn't said a word and I'm unsure how much of my inner turmoil she's picked up on.

I keep watching her changing gears – first up, then down as we approach an intersection and up again as she makes the turn, accelerating.

The familiar movements of driving and shifting gears brings me back to myself, even though it's not me making the motions. It's strangely soothing to watch someone else do it, to be a passenger being carried along, not having to make decisions.

My phone buzzes against the plastic where it's resting. I don't look, but Hollie does.

"Is everything okay?" She's trying to look at me while also watching the road. I'm still looking at her hand, but can see the rest of her from the corner of my eye. Concern is written into her posture and the quick glances she's sending me.

I clear my throat. "Yeah." The word comes out rough and not at all believable. I clear my throat again. "Yeah, everything's fine. It's someone I don't want to talk to right now. It's nothing urgent, but could we maybe talk about something else?"

She looks at me properly for a second, as if assessing my mental stability. I make eye contact briefly, trying to convey how desperately I need to talk about something else without appearing like I do. She turns back to the road.

"Sure. Um … How'd you like Harley?"

I exhale, dropping my head back against the headrest. "He was cool. Not sure my ass agrees though."

She laughs lightly and the sound helps me breathe a little easier. "It'll get better, if you do it enough." The gold bracelet on her wrist glints in the light and I watch it shifting with her movements as I slide into the conversation, letting her words bring me back to the moment and myself.

I've only known this girl a day – not even that, really – but she's making it very easy to want to be around her.

I like being with her. She makes me feel like myself, like the old me, not the strange eerie version of myself I've been using to go through the motions.

The past few months I've been trapped, unable to find the person I used to be, but Hollie, with her overwhelming kindness and gentle strength, makes me remember what being me used to feel like. I can talk to her, and sure, it's only mundane things like my first attempt at riding a horse since I was six, but for a while there I thought I'd completely lost the ability to have a conversation with anyone.

My parents were going spare over me. They know what happened to Luke, but they don't *really* know what happened to Luke, so while they understood I was upset about my best friend, they couldn't fathom how I'd become this totally different person.

I overheard them talking one night a few weeks ago, when I'd got up for a late-night wander around the house. It was something I'd taken to doing when I couldn't sleep, so it's happened a lot since December. I wandered aimlessly from room to room in the dark, looking for some form of peace, if only for a few moments.

My parents didn't know I was wandering that night. I'm not sure if they knew I did it at all. I heard them talking as I passed their bedroom, where the door was slightly open.

"What are we going to do about him?" Mum said. There was a pause and my dad murmured something, but it was too muffled to hear.

"I don't know what happened." Mum's voice cracked as she spoke, the words splintering like my heart was. "He won't talk to anyone, he doesn't play anymore, won't even listen to music. The school's concerned already and the year's barely started."

I didn't hear any more; I didn't stay to listen. Without my conscious thought or effort, my feet carried me silently back down the hall to my room where I closed the door as quietly as I could. I sat on the floor for hours, back pressed against the door, staring at my guitar in the corner. The guitar I saved every cent for years to buy, the guitar I played every single day until my fingers were blistered and sore, the guitar my mother noticed I hadn't touched in months.

What's the point when you don't have a drummer to play with?

Hollie's phone rings and interrupts our conversation. I'm so relieved it's not mine.

A voice fills the car, echoing through her hands-free system.

"Hollie, you gorgeous thing!" the male voice booms. "Please don't tell me you've stood me up. My heart can't take it."

I raise an eyebrow at Hollie, who's playing it off like she isn't heading to a date. She's grinning and shaking her head, a touch of pink highlighting her cheeks.

"Hey, Danny. Before you say anything else ridiculous, you're on speaker and I'm not alone." She turns to me with a roll of her eyes and mutters, "Sorry, he's an idiot."

"I heard that," Danny's voice cuts in. This must be the guy I've seen her with at school, the tall one with the blonde hair. I wasn't sure if they were a couple, but this phone call is sure confirming it.

"Well, it's true. Anyway, I'm on my way to you. I won't be long. Promise."

"Okay, cool. So who are you with? Who's preventing you being with me already?"

Hollie groans audibly. "Seriously, stop being so dramatic." But she says it with a laugh, and I know there's more to this relationship than just friends.

"I'm with Beth's nephew, Jonathan. He's the new guy at school."

"Oh, right. Hey, Jonathan," Danny says to me.

"Uh, hi," I say back, super awkwardly. "Yep, I'm the new guy." Sigh. I'm sick of being the new guy already. It's only been two days. I wonder how long it'll be before I'm part of the scenery.

"Is it you with that sweet green Holden? And if so, what on earth are you doing risking life and limb letting Hollie drive you anywhere in her tin can?"

I laugh and catch a glimpse of Hollie's face, which is burning red. She's probably remembering our initial meeting that risked life and limb because of Hollie's driving, or actually my stupidity. I can tell Danny's teasing is undercut with genuine affection though, and I know Hollie knows it too, because despite the blush she's grinning.

"Yeah, that's mine, but Hollie gave me a ride home last night and she's giving me a ride to pick up my car."

"Geez, what'd you have to do to get her to do that? Considering it's delaying her laying eyes on my charming face."

"He rode Harley for me," Hollie cuts in, giving me a sideways grin.

"He rode *Harley*?" His laugh echoes around the confines of the car. "I wish I'd seen that."

"Don't worry, I've got pictures."

And now I know why that sideways grin looked so wicked.

"What's wrong with Harley?" I ask, confused. "He was cool."

"Yeah, but he's little," Danny says, "and you're not exactly short, right? Did you even have to take your feet off the ground? You'd have been better on literally any other horse."

"Alaska was the other option," Hollie says, still grinning. Her whole demeanour seems to have changed since Danny called. It's like her happiness has been turned up to full beam.

"Yeah, well, that was a lot further to fall," I mutter.

"That's true, but Alaska's a sweetie, like Harley and Milo. They're all good horses. Your aunt has good taste and I'm not even a horse kind of guy."

"Yeah, but the things you'll do for me, right, Danny?"

"You got it, gorgeous. I'll catch you soon, right? Things to do, people to see, all that."

Hollie releases a gentle laugh. "I'll be there soon, you complete fool."

"Only for you, my love. Catch you later, Jonathan."

And with that, he's gone. The call ends and the stereo starts playing again. Hollie lets out a breath then looks to me.

"Sorry about him. He is, quite frankly, a fool. But…" She shrugs. "He's Danny, I guess. It's how he is. I adore him." There's a look in her eye that betrays the lightness of her tone, like there's more to what he means to her, but I can't figure it out.

"He seems cool." I choose my words carefully, unsure what I'm supposed to say. There's a strange twisting in my gut, like disappointment.

It's ridiculous.

She's a nice person, and she's never been flirty or anything more than friendly with me in the very brief time we've known each other. Being nice to someone doesn't mean they're into you; it simply means they're nice. And why would she see me as anything other than a jerk and a nuisance? Not that I'm even capable of having friends, let alone anything else. I shut my brain down.

"He is. I think you'd like him." She gives me that smile of hers again. "You can hang out with us at school or whatever … if you want." It sounds like a question, but I'm not sure how to answer.

She indicates and pulls swiftly to the curb, and I'm looking at the back bumper of my car.

"Yeah, that sounds good. Thanks for the ride." I climb out and pause, holding the door open for a minute, trying to think what to say. "Have fun with Danny." Then I shut the door and head for my car. I hope I didn't come across as snarky as I feel, because I shouldn't feel snarky at all.

Hollie waits, her car idling as I start the engine of mine, its loud rumble a stark contrast to her little hatchback's purr. I ease into gear and at the end of the street turn in the opposite direction to her.

CHAPTER 9

Hollie

"HEY, GORGEOUS."

Dan slides into the passenger seat and his eyes flick over me. "Ooh, you're looking fancy. Is that for my benefit, or the new guy?" He waggles his eyebrows at me and laughs as my face darkens.

"Maybe I wanted to wear something pretty," I grumble. Which is the truth. I'm told making an effort in how I present myself to the world makes a difference to how I feel, so I thought today I'd do more than go through the motions. But the comments from the two people I've seen are making me doubt my choice. Maybe it's too much.

"And pretty it is," Dan says, and I know he's sincere. "So tell me about this Jonathan." He turns to me, a twinkle in his eye.

"God, you're truly annoying," I say. "There isn't much to tell. He's moved in with Beth, apparently to help her on the farm, except I'm not sure he's done a day of physical labour in his life. He's a bit of a city boy. Anyway, he drank too much last night and I gave him a ride home. He was a jackass this morning, begged forgiveness, did some farm work, rode Harley and then I took him back to his car. That's it." I shrug, trying to convey nonchalance.

That was exactly it. Nothing more.

Except it doesn't really feel like it.

I think of the last words Jonathan said to me, and the feeling they caused in my body. They struck me like ice. I wonder if he meant them the way I received them, or if my brain was playing tricks on me again. I'm never truly sure anymore of the meaning behind what people say.

I can still feel Dan's gaze. He's probably assessing how far he can push me on this. I keep my eyes on the road, hoping he'll drop it.

He does.

"So, where to today?" He pulls out his phone as he asks and I know he's pulling up the stupid list he keeps on there, nicknamed 'Hollie's Bucket List'. It's nothing as dire as the words make it sound. It's simply a list of things I'd like to try, or that I enjoy, and he uses it to bully me into doing them.

"Food," I say. "I need food before I can even think of anything else."

"To Chester's then! Onward!" He grins and flops back into the seat, his arm thrust forward in a clear signal. I grin back at him and head for our favourite café. This is what I love about being around Dan. He knows my limits, he knows when he can push me beyond them, and he always, always knows how to lighten the mood. Being around him is easy, even when nothing else is.

I've been friends with Dan since our first year of high school, in that strange way you slowly get to know people you're forced to spend hours with every day.

Everyone came in from different schools and it took a while for the different social groups to shift and change, relegating each of us to our specific friendships. Dan ended up on the periphery of mine.

My crush on him burst to life the minute I saw him smile, which may have been the first time I ever laid eyes on him. A stupid crush I told Kaitlin about in an even stupider moment of my life.

But honestly, I don't know how anyone could not instantly fall a little bit in love with the guy. He's one of those innately charming people, but never boastful, never arrogant. He's tall, with crazy blond hair tumbling around his ears – a dirty golden halo – and a contagious grin that lets loose a single dimple.

It's his eyes though, that I find most captivating. A deep, warm brown, they express every feeling, smile, laugh or frown that crosses his face.

I'd look into them forever, but it gets a little awkward after a while.

Our social calendars crossed, our classes crossed and we were friends. Maybe I was interested in being more than friends. But then my life, or more specifically, my brain, got in the way.

The darkness came and it swallowed me whole.

It was Dan who found me.

I'd been away from school for three days. I texted Kaitlin and told her I was sick but didn't elaborate. I didn't tell her that getting out of bed had grown more and more difficult, and that I simply couldn't do it anymore. I didn't tell her that the thought of food made me nauseated. I didn't tell her that I spent those three days lying in bed in the dark with tears leaking from my eyes and my mother wringing her hands over me, wondering where this sudden "flu" had come from.

The afternoon of the third day, Dan came to visit. I was in a right state. I told Mum to send him away, that I didn't want to see him. She tried to get me up to shower and at least say hello to him, but I couldn't. I told her to tell him to go away, then buried myself under my blankets again.

But this is Daniel we're talking about. He is equal parts stubborn and charismatic. He charmed my mother into letting him into my room. As I felt someone lower themself onto the edge of my bed I expected to feel my mother's hand on my shoulder, but this hand was different. It was bigger and stronger.

"How're you doing, Hollie?" he asked in his deep, soothing voice. I started to cry again, the tears leaking from my eyes to slip down my face.

"You shouldn't be here," I sniffled, peeking over my duvet at him. "I might be contagious."

His beautiful brown eyes were filled with worry. It was such a stark contrast to his usual easy smile.

"Oh, you lovely thing. I don't think what you're going through is contagious." He pushed my hair back from my face, smoothing it down, working his fingers gently through a tangle.

"What do you mean? How do you know what I've got? I don't even know." I was suddenly angry, filled with rage that he could walk in here like nothing was the matter and know what was going on with me. It was a brief second, then it evaporated, because being angry was too damn exhausting.

"I have an idea, but you need to go see a doctor." He paused for a long moment and I could see him debating if he should tell me more. "I think it's depression."

I still remember how numb I felt when he said it. My mind tried to process the words but failed.

"I don't have the slightest thing to be depressed about," I said.

He shrugged, like that was nothing. "Sometimes it's not about that. But you're tired a lot, you've stopped hanging out with us as much, and sometimes when you do it's like you aren't there at all. Plus you barely eat, and you quit riding – something you've loved for as long as I've known you. They're all symptoms, Hollie."

"How do you know any of this?" I pushed myself to sitting, clenching my blankets against myself like a shield. My brain was still trying to work through what he'd said. Did I do all those things?

He shrugged again. "I've seen it before and I notice things. I notice you, Hollie." He said it with a little smile, then reached out to wrap his arms around me, lack of basic hygiene and all. "I talked to your mum about it when I came in. She's making an appointment to see your doctor."

I allowed him to pull me close. It was too much effort to pull away. But he was warm and solid and I felt completely and utterly safe.

"Will you come with me?" I whispered to the fabric of his shirt.

"Of course. Anything you need, Hollie. Anything."

Then he sat and held me while more tears ran down my face for what felt like an eternity.

Eventually, I found a tiny bit of strength – strength he'd no doubt given me – and pushed myself away.

"I need a shower," I said, trying not to think of the state of me or my room.

"A good start."

Dan helped me up, led me to the bathroom and started the shower. Before he left, he pressed a kiss to my forehead and whispered, "You can do this" in my ear.

The next morning he skipped second period to go with me and Mum to the doctor, who confirmed my depression and recommended a therapist.

Dan's been with me ever since. At some stage the crush fizzled out. I don't think I had the energy for it while battling back the fogginess that had overtaken all aspects of my life. Instead, he became my best friend.

When I pull into my driveway later that evening I'm tired but smiling. It was a long day, what with getting up at six to go riding then spending the rest of the day with Dan.

We ate three helpings of curly fries and sliders at Chester's, then went bowling.

We laughed until our sides hurt at the pictures I'd covertly snapped of Jonathan perched on Harley, who really was far too small for someone as tall as Jonathan. It's not that the sturdy little horse can't bear his weight; it's that Jonathan's legs are so long it looked clownish. Dan didn't push me further about any possible crush on Jonathan, but he did ask about him.

"Why'd he move here?"

I shrugged in response. "No idea. Maybe to help Beth? God knows she needs it. Maybe he's in witness protection? Maybe he's in trouble with the law? Or a tragic accident killed his entire family?" I paused. "Yikes, I hope not any of those last ones. Man, that got dark."

"Sure did, Holls. You took it there." He chewed thoughtfully on a fry. "He's awfully good looking though, right?"

I shrug again. "If you like arrogant jerks, sure."

"Oh, come on, Holls!" He flicked the crumbs on his fingers at me, laughing. "The guy was hungover and found some random in his house at some god-awful time of the morning going through his washing. Give him a break."

"I did, and drove him to his car, remember?"

He snorted. "Yeah sure, after you made him ride Harley."

I laughed. "He said he wanted to help."

The hours passed so quickly, then it was time to head home and have dinner with Mum, the first time I would have seen her all day. I dropped Dan off and considered stopping by Beth's. As I approached the turnoff to her road I found myself slowing the car.

Then I caught myself. I had no conceivable reason to go back again.

I had made sure everything was taken care of that morning, and I'd told Beth I wouldn't be back. Still, the pull had made me slow the car further and flick the indicator on.

I thought of Jonathan. His ruffled dark hair: the way he shoved his hand into it, his fingers tangling in the strands; the easy way he carried himself with that swaggering confidence. I flicked the indicator lever again, switching it off, and accelerated past the intersection. I was not going back to hang around swooning over a boy.

CHAPTER 10

Hollie

JONATHAN'S CAR is in the carpark when I arrive at school on Monday morning. I catch sight of the metallic green through a throng of students.

I didn't see him at Beth's yesterday. There was no sign of Beth and Thea either, so maybe they'd all gone somewhere together.

I took Milo for a long ride over the hills, leaving a note on Beth's door to let her know where we were heading, just in case.

She doesn't have a problem with me riding when she isn't home, but she has expressly forbidden me from jumping when no one is around. That rule is fine by me. I'm barely brave enough to do it with someone keeping an eye on me.

I thought I heard the low grumble of Jonathan's car while I was in the back of the barn prepping horse feed for the next day, but by the time I emerged there was no sign of anyone.

I felt strangely disappointed that he hadn't come to say hello. But why would he? I wished this stupid fluttery feeling would leave me alone.

As I left, I poked my head into the kitchen to catch up with Beth, but still no Jonathan. The only sign he was even living there was a hoodie tossed over the back of a chair. I chased away the disappointment again.

Then last night, while emptying my weekend's worth of clothes, riding boots and fast food rubbish from my car, I found his phone. It must have slipped from the centre console down the side of the seat at some point on Saturday. The lock screen was filled with missed calls and messages. I plugged it into my charger so he'd have some battery power left to reply to them all.

Now, I slip his phone into my jeans pocket and slide my bag over my shoulder, heading towards the classrooms. I have no idea how I'll find Jonathan, but I have to start somewhere.

It turns out he's extremely easy to find. He's leaning against the front of his car, surrounded by a group of guys.

My heart skips and I appreciate how good he looks in dark wash jeans and a grey jacket. His hair falls forward and he pushes it back in that strangely captivating gesture of his.

My heart sinks as I take in the guys standing with him: Jake Daly and Simon Michaels, along with the rest of their little crew of idiots. It's a nasty thought to have, but honestly, they're crass and rude and disruptive. They're the kind of guys who don't realise laughing *at* someone isn't the same as laughing *with* them.

I normally avoid them as much as possible, but if I don't give Jonathan his phone now I might not catch up with him again today. I can't handle the guilt, especially with the number of missed calls on his phone. Someone *really* wants to talk to him.

I pull the phone out and fiddle with it. My steps have slowed, but I force my feet to keep moving. If they stop it's likely they'll never start again. I edge between his car and the one parked next to it. Jonathan's facing away from me, laughing, and I hesitate. I don't want the attention this group is going to give me.

But it's too late.

Simon spots me hovering at the edge of the group. He raises his eyebrows and gives me a suggestive look. I glance away and will Jonathan to turn to me. I force another step.

"Uh, hey." I manage to get the words out, my voice coming steadier than I'd expected.

Jonathan turns and the smile drops off his face. It's gone for barely a moment before it's replaced by another smile. A different one.

But I can't tell if the change is good or bad. I can't tell if he's happy to see me, or if I'm simply intruding on his life a little more.

"Hey," he says easily, and jerks his head towards the school building closest to us, a wordless *Walk with me?* I nod and step out from between the cars.

"See you later, guys," he calls back to the group, and I catch sight of several smirks on smug faces.

Fabulous.

Someone wolf whistles. Another voice calls out, "Hey, Johnny! You were holding out on us!"

The group breaks into raucous laughter and I cringe. They're behaving pretty much as I anticipated.

Jonathan groans. "I'm sorry. They're idiots."

"Yeah, but they're your friends." I shrug and hold out his

phone. "I found this in my car. Um, there's quite a few missed calls."

He takes the phone, a look of both relief and regret on his face.

"Thought my life had got quiet." He mutters the words under his breath, and I wonder if I was supposed to hear them. "Thanks," he says, louder, so I was definitely supposed to hear that. "And I'd use the term 'friends' really loosely where they're concerned."

"Weren't you at the party with them?"

He nods. "Sort of, but we both know how that ended." He sighs, then seems to shake it off. "Have a nice weekend? The rest of it I mean, after I saw you?"

"Yeah, I did." I try to smile at him, trying to forget the way his last words to me on Saturday affected me. "Did you? Go somewhere nice yesterday?"

He looks at me sideways. "You stalking me or something?"

I'm surprised when I laugh. "No, but I came to take Milo out and no one was around."

"Yeah, I took Beth to the supermarket and we bought some plants and lightbulbs. It was very exciting. I'm suddenly a middle-aged dad." He's smiling through the sarcasm and it's nice to see. For some reason I keep remembering the Jonathan I found sitting in the gutter, broken and sad.

He stops abruptly and fishes his phone back out of his pocket. The display is lit up. The name Kristen and a picture of a dark-haired girl poking tongues at the camera flashes on the screen.

Jonathan groans. "I'd better answer this one," he says, not looking up at me.

"Sure," I say, angling away from him, continuing towards class. "I'll see you round somewhere."

He nods distractedly, already lifting the phone up to his ear.

"Hey, Kris," I hear him say as I walk away.

I turn back and watch him for a moment before I reach the building.

"Were you hanging out with the new guy?" Kaitlin appears beside me. I start in surprise. Either she's learning to be a spy or I was way too caught up in thoughts of Jonathan to notice her approach.

I'm less than overjoyed at the truth of the second option.

"Geez, don't sneak up on people!" I say, regardless of that truth. She could have stomped up behind me riding an elephant and I wouldn't have noticed.

"I didn't sneak up," she says, indignant. "It is not my fault at all that you were distracted from my arrival." She pauses, a sly smile slipping onto her face. "Got to say though, I don't blame you."

I glance over at her. She's watching Jonathan, an appraising gleam in her eye. I raise an eyebrow. "What about Connor?"

"What about him? You know I'm all into that, but I mean … look at that guy…" She turns back to me and the gleam is still there. "Anyway. You were talking to him, yes? Tell me everything!"

I laugh. Somehow I've landed myself with two best friends who behave more like puppies than people most of the time. Their enthusiasm for everything is so terribly over the top.

"So that," I say, tilting my head in Jonathan's direction, "is Beth's nephew Jonathan. He moved here on Wednesday, so Beth has an extra pair of hands."

"That's very sweet of him," Kaitlin says quietly. She knows the ride Beth's been on.

"It is. Anyway, I met him on Friday as I was leaving the party and I gave him a ride home."

"*Hollie!*" She rounds on me, so unexpectedly I'm forced to step back. "You got into a car with a guy you didn't know? Jesus, I thought you knew better."

I shrug. I do know better. Which is why the whole situation was so unreal. The truth was, once I started talking to him I didn't want the conversation to end. Even when I should have felt awkward and uncomfortable and possibly even unsafe, I didn't – which of course means I should have been even more vigilant, though Kaitlin doesn't know I texted Dan to tell him I was giving Jonathan a ride home. She doesn't need to know that part.

"I know, I know," I say. "I did tell someone I was letting him into my car so they'd know where to look if I went missing. But he wasn't at all sleazy, not even the tiniest bit. He helped around the farm on Saturday and even got on Harley."

Kaitlin snorts in laughter and I let out a breath when I realise she isn't going to ask who I told. I pull my phone out and show her the photo evidence of Jonathan on Harley and she laughs even harder.

"Then I drove him back to his car and that was that."

She studies me and I work hard to keep my face expressionless.

"And that was that?" she says slowly. "Really?" She's got her smirk back. It's the same face she gets when she's talking about Dan, and god, I can't do this with her again.

"That's that," I say, starting towards school.

I don't tell her the rest of it. The despair in him when I

found him, the angry outburst in the laundry, the apologies, his reaction to his phone ringing.

There's more to him than meets the eye. I know it. But I also know what it's like to want to hide that part of you from the world, so I'm not going to tell Kaitlin.

Whatever is going on with Jonathan is his business, not hers.

CHAPTER 11

Jonathan

"JOHNNY! ABOUT TIME!"

Kristen's voice carries down the line and into my eardrum. I hold the phone away from my head and fumble with the volume control.

"Sorry," I say. "I left my phone in someone's car. I've just got it back."

"Someone? Someone who? Have you made a friend?"

"Geez, Kris, calm down."

My mind wanders to Hollie, and so does my gaze as I notice her standing near the doors into the classroom block, talking to her brunette friend.

I'm not sure if I've made a friend or not. I know I like being around her, but that doesn't really mean anything. I give myself a mental shake. It doesn't matter right now anyway.

"She's riding Beth's horses and she gave me a ride somewhere. That's all."

"Ooh, a she! What's she like?"

"Seriously Kris, what's up?" I say, exasperation lacing my tone. I need to get to the point and get this over with.

I knew I'd have to answer her calls at some point. Of all the people I left behind, Kristen was the least likely to let me go without a fight.

It's not her fault. She never wanted any of this and was never any part of it, but she's still a painful reminder of the past.

Which is something I'd prefer not to think about.

At all.

Ever.

"Nothing's up," she says. "Why do you ask?"

"Because you've called me like fifteen times. I haven't even made it to the messages yet and you've called me again."

"Oh." She pauses. "No. Nothing's up. I wanted to check in, that's all. It's weird you not being here. I miss you."

"I miss you too, little sis." I take a breath, fortifying myself for the lie that's coming. "I need to be here."

Once the words are out I realise it's not even a lie. I do need to be here, only not for the reasons I told her and the rest of my family.

"I know … it's just the timing. It could have been better."

I don't say anything for a moment. What Kristen doesn't realise is that the timing was perfect for me.

Yeah, I miss her, which is weird for a guy to say about his little sister, but we've always been close.

I miss our parents too. But having to go back to school after a summer of avoiding anything and anyone from before made me realise how badly I needed to get out.

I was trapped, and Beth really does need help. I'm more convinced of that now than ever after hearing how much Thea doesn't like to sleep.

"Yeah, I suppose. You'll have to take it up with Beth."

She laughs a little. "Yeah, maybe. How is she?"

"She's good. Tired, though. Thea's cute but doesn't seem to be much of a fan of sleeping."

She laughs even more at that, then it trails off into a slightly awkward pause. "Are you going to ask how he is?" Her tone is suddenly serious. She's led me right into this.

The grief, the guilt, smacks me right in the face, again.

"Kris, I've got to go. My battery's dying. We'll catch up properly soon, though. I promise." The words come in a flood, a dam bursting and spilling over, wiping away anything in its path, leaving no way to return to the conversation she tried to lead me into.

I hear her sigh on the other end of the line. "All right, Johnny. I love you."

"Love you too. Bye, Kris." My voice cracks on her name and I jab at the screen, scrabbling to end the call, then shove the phone into my pocket.

I reach out and grab a verandah post nearby and lean on it, waiting for my breathing to settle. As I get a handle on my emotions, my phone vibrates.

I pull it out again. I can't decide if knowing or not knowing is worse.

> Kristen: So you know, he's doing well. Things
> are looking really good. He misses you though.
> I can't believe you didn't tell him you were
> leaving. Maybe you should answer one of his
> calls sometime too…

I shake my head, trying to force away the tears blurring my eyes. I power the phone off and bury it in the depths of my bag.

I bury the thoughts too, the memories and the feelings.

I shove them down and head into class. Hopefully the tedium of school will be enough to distract me.

The day drags, my mind torturing me with memories.

I think a lot about Kristen's text.

I know she was trying to help, but she has no idea what's happened and how I can't go back.

I didn't know how to tell him I was leaving, so I said nothing at all. I don't think my radio silence will be surprising to him anymore.

I wonder if I should text him, maybe even call him. His name was on the list of notifications that came up on my screen, but I don't read the messages. After months of avoidance, I'm worried what they might say.

Of course I want to text him, to call him, to have him as part of my life again. But I don't know how to bridge the gap.

"Gap" seems like an understatement. It's a gaping, bottomless ravine.

I want more than anything for things to be the way they were before, but they never can be and somehow I have to learn to live with that.

He has enough to deal with without my dramas.

No, I can't do that to him.

It'll be easier for Luke without me there.

Easier for everyone, eventually.

I pull into Beth's driveway and feel the tension in my body ease slightly.

At least here I don't have to try quite so hard to hide.

It's funny I still call this Beth's place. It is, but I suppose it's my home now too. I park my car in her garage, beside her beaten up ute, then head inside.

I find her curled up on the couch, fast asleep. Thea is in the little cot thing Beth calls a bassinet in the corner of the lounge, awake but quiet. She locks eyes with me as I peer in to check on her. I freeze, then slowly try to back away. She makes a small squawking noise as I ease out of her vision, and it makes me freeze again.

Beth is so knocked out. I know she didn't get much sleep again last night. I make a rash decision and scoop the baby out of her bed.

She gurgles, grabbing at my hair, giving me a gummy smile. I scribble a note to Beth, leaving it in the bassinet. The contraption Beth uses to carry Thea around is lying on the kitchen table and I grab that on my way back out the door.

Hollie has arrived in the few minutes I've been inside. She's already in the arena, moving around the poles she uses for jumping. I approach the fence with Thea in my arms.

"Hey," I call out.

She doesn't respond.

My stomach drops. I haven't seen her since this morning, when she gave my phone back.

I wonder what the idiots I was with said to her, or about her.

They all think we hooked up. Why else would I leave a party so early? How else would she get my phone?

I hope they haven't said anything to her. I hope even more that if they did, she doesn't believe that I told them any of that shit.

I realise she's moving weirdly. I can't quite figure out what she's doing, and I watch her for a moment before a grin spreads across my face.

I can't help it.

She's dancing.

And singing.

Sort of.

She's not exactly singing well, but I suppose it's still classed as singing.

She adjusts the jump in front of her, lowering the height, while shaking her hips to whatever beat she's listening to. She takes a few steps, then spins.

She catches sight of me and freezes. Her face flushes a deep glowing red.

I have to admit I love watching her blush. I shouldn't, but I do.

She pulls AirPods out and tucks them into her pocket.

"Hey," I say again.

"Um, hi." She fiddles with the end of her plait.

"Good song, huh?" I'm fighting to keep the grin off my face. I'm pretty sure I'm losing.

Hollie nods stiffly and comes across the arena to us.

"Hey, baby girl," she croons to Thea in the same voice I've heard her use with the horses. Thea reaches out and grasps her finger and they smile at each other. "You gonna come be a horse girl today, huh? You wanna go riding? Mummy will have to get you a pony, won't she?" Thea gurgles and Hollie grins up at me, the blush fading from her cheeks. "God, she's cute."

"Yeah, except when it's two am and she's been crying for three hours. No wonder Beth is crashed out right now." I hold out the bundle of buckles and straps in my hand. I've seen it on

Beth so I know it turns into a baby carrier somehow. "Do you know how to work this contraption?"

Hollie takes it from me, untangling the straps and turning it this way and that, studying it.

"Can't be worse than a bridle, right?" She climbs over the fence, jumping lightly down to the ground beside me. I have an almost unbearable urge to reach out and steady her.

She doesn't need it, but suddenly my hands yearn to touch her. It's a good thing I'm holding a baby or maybe I would.

Hollie steps behind me and I go to turn towards her, but a light touch on my shoulder stops me. Her hand is warm, but it feels like she's scorched my skin through my t-shirt.

My stomach lurches.

Then she reaches her arms right around my waist and I almost fall over.

I force myself to hold still as she passes a strap from one hand to the other, and just like that her arms are gone from around me. The buckle clicks together behind my back. I let out my breath, slowly, not wanting her to know I was holding it.

Her hand touches my shoulder again and this time I turn as she pushes gently. She lifts the front of the carrier, helping me settle Thea into it. Hollie slides the straps over my arms and turns me again to click the last buckle into place.

Thea is suddenly snug and secure against my chest. She's a reassuringly warm weight, anchoring me, and a stark contrast to the fire and adrenaline coursing through my veins. Every spot on my body Hollie has touched tingles, even the places she softly brushed, her fingers barely felt.

"Does Beth know you have her?" Hollie's question brings

me back from the brink of either passing out or reaching out for her, which I expect really wouldn't go down well.

I nod. "I left a note in the bassinet. I didn't want Beth to freak out if she woke up, but this little thing was awake and I thought her mum might need as much rest as she can get." I wiggle one of Thea's feet. It fits snugly into the palm of my hand and I marvel at how tiny people start out. "Especially if we have another repeat of last night…" I sigh. "And the night before that." The thought of it makes me tired and I drag my hand across my face.

"Sounds like you could do with some sleep too."

Hollie is standing in front of me again, her hand resting against Thea's back. She's glancing between me and the baby, alternating pulling funny faces and looking at me with concern in her eyes.

I shrug. "I'll be fine. I'm getting way more than Beth."

"Well, let me know if I can help." She pauses, then seems to come to a decision. "In the meantime, wanna see what Harley can really do?"

I nod and Hollie strides away across the gravel yard to the barn. She smiles back at me over her shoulder, and like I'm under a spell I follow without making a conscious decision to take a single step.

Harley ambles over to us when we reach the paddock. Hollie smiles, crooning to him and scratching him behind his ears as she slips the halter on. He stands patiently as she saddles him. I stand back, hesitant to get too close with Thea strapped to me.

Harley nickers and stretches out his nose.

"It's okay," Hollie says. "They know each other."

Thea's little hand is stretching out from the side of the

carrier and I step forward so her chubby fingers can touch Harley's soft muzzle. Thea gurgles and it almost sounds like a laugh.

"She really is a horse girl, isn't she?"

Hollie grins. "She sure is, like her mummy. I'm not sure there was any chance she'd be anything else."

When Harley is ready to go we head back to the arena together.

I should be doing something. Something helpful. I should be working. But I don't know how to do anything with a baby tied to my chest.

So instead I climb up and sit on the railings. Thea has settled, snuggled in against me. It's a feeling I can't describe, but it's definitely not bad. It's kind of weirdly relaxing and reassuring.

Hollie makes her final preparations – checking the saddle, adjusting a couple of straps – then takes a couple of steps back from Harley. She takes a deep breath, then one giant step, and throws herself into the air. Her leg slides up and over the saddle and she settles herself on Harley's back.

"What the…" I'm gaping at her, staring with my mouth open and no words coming out. I've never seen anything like it in my life.

Hollie glances over at me, a touch of pink finding her cheeks again. "He's small enough for me to do that. Definitely couldn't do it with Alaska or Milo."

I continue to stare. It's like she doesn't think it's a big deal she jumped onto a horse's back. From the ground.

Hollie nudges Harley and they move forward. They work their way around the arena: up and down, changing directions and gaits, taking it slowly and warming up.

After a while Hollie starts taking Harley over the jumps she set up earlier. They're much lower than what Alaska was jumping the other day, but I suppose Harley is much smaller. The pair handle them with ease. There isn't a single moment they falter.

I feel a shift in the air and turn to see Beth climbing up next to me on the railings. She peers into the baby carrier and checks on her daughter. She's fast asleep, her little fist resting beside her cheek, clutching tightly to my shirt.

"Thanks for taking her for a bit," Beth murmurs. "It was a long night."

"Sounded like it," I whisper back. "She was awake when I went in. I didn't want her to wake you."

Beth smiles, the exhaustion still pulling at her features, and pats my shoulder. "I struck it lucky with you as my nephew."

Heat finds my face and I duck my head, pretending to check Thea again.

I don't say anything. There's nothing to say. I'm not sure I can remember the last time anyone thought they were lucky to have me in their life.

"You're going to get a real show now," Beth says, gesturing towards Hollie. "Have you seen what she can do?"

"I saw her jump with apparently no effort involved. And I've seen her riding Alaska, if that's what you mean?"

Beth shakes her head. "You've seen her schooling a low-level show jumper and warming up. She's been training Harley to be a pony club mount, but his real talent is mounted games."

I have no idea what Beth's talking about, so I return my gaze to the girl and pony working their way up and down the arena. After a few lengths Hollie heads in our direction and eases Harley to a stop beside me. She fiddles with the saddle a little and adjusts her stirrups so her legs hang long down Harley's sides. Then she knots the reins and lays them across his neck.

"You want a starter?" Beth asks, climbing down from the rail.

Hollie nods and settles herself into the saddle before urging Harley to the far side of the arena. Beth collects a flag from a barrel in the centre and drags a line across the sandy surface.

Hollie sets Harley into a gallop and races the length of the arena, pulling up abruptly at the end before spinning him round and charging back. Her plait swings out behind her as she crouches over the pony's neck, standing in the stirrups. All she does to slide Harley to a stop is sit back in the saddle. That's what it looks like from where I'm sitting, anyway.

"Ready?" Beth calls out and Hollie walks Harley to the line. His head is up, nostrils flaring and ears pointed forward. He skips a little but she holds him steady, resting her palm against his neck. Her gaze is laser-focussed on the arena in front of her.

Beth holds the flag aloft, counts down and drops the flag to the ground.

In an instant Harley is off the line, tail streaming like a dark ribbon behind him. He weaves easily through a line of poles pushed into the arena ground. As he reaches the last pole Hollie sits back and looks for the start line, and the little pony spins on his haunches before powering for home.

The whole thing is over in seconds.

"Woah," I breathe, speaking to no one. Hollie pulls Harley up at the end of the arena and comes to a stop in front of

Beth, rubbing his neck. Her face is split with a grin, her cheeks pink again, this time with exertion.

"Good job," I hear Beth say before she hands Hollie some road cones.

Hollie sets up, then races to move flags between the different cones. On the next run she gallops to the end, jumps off the moving horse, grabs something off the ground, jumps back on the still-moving horse and drops whatever she's picked up into a bucket.

I've never seen anything like it in my life.

The speed and agility is something I can barely comprehend. This Harley isn't even close to the quiet little pony I rode two days ago.

And this Hollie, the fierce-as-fuck one who's leaping on and off a galloping horse like it's a casual Sunday stroll, is nothing like the one I thought I knew.

I thought I had her figured out.

I most definitely do not.

Finally, when Harley's coat is dark with sweat and he's puffing hard, Hollie calls an end to their session.

"Such a good boy," Hollie is saying as she leads him over to me.

"That was insane," I say, falling into step beside her. "What even was it?"

"Mounted games," she replies. "A series of races. It's all done on speed but you've got to do a whole bunch of different things, like picking things up and dropping them in buckets, or moving flags. Lots of speed, agility and hand-eye coordination." She turns back to Harley and rubs him on the nose. "This little dude's a star. I'm hoping he'll go to a kid who's keen on that kind of thing. Though he would be awesome for just about anyone."

"What do you mean go to a kid?" I ask, not sure I really want to know the answer.

"He's for sale," she says, a tinge of sadness to her voice. "He's a bit small for Beth, but she couldn't resist taking him on. He was pretty green and not particularly well cared for, because his owners got a fright and were scared of him. We've been working to get him ready to be awesome for a kid at pony club."

I nod slowly. It all makes sense and it doesn't surprise me at all that Beth couldn't resist taking in a lost soul, or at least a misunderstood one.

She took *me* in, after all.

I give the little horse a pat. Even from our brief acquaintance, I'm pretty fond of the little guy and it'll be sad to see him go.

"Is there much interest? Will he sell fast?"

"There's been a little bit, but he hasn't been out anywhere so no one really knows about him. I'm riding him at an event in a couple of weeks so hopefully we get some interest there."

Hollie heads for the barn, leading the slightly less puffed Harley behind her.

I reach out and touch her arm. It's the lightest touch, enough to catch her attention, but I feel the heat sizzle through my fingertips, and it's not heat caused by her charging around an arena.

"You are really good at this horse thing, you know," I say quietly, holding her gaze. When I asked her about it on Saturday she brushed it off, like it was no big deal.

But it is a big deal.

"It's all Harley. I'm only here for the ride," she mumbles, breaking eye contact and scuffing one of her boots in the dirt.

"That's completely untrue. You're amazing." And then like I'm some super confident, have-it-all-together king of guy, I gently squeeze her arm and walk away.

I make it about three steps before I start mentally face-palming myself.

"God, Thea," I whisper to the baby who's still snuggled up asleep against my chest. "Your big cousin's a total idiot, isn't he?"

CHAPTER 12

Hollie

KAITLIN'S SITTING on my front step when I pull into the driveway.

She's scrolling her phone and doesn't even glance up as I climb out of my car.

It's not completely unheard of that Kaitlin turns up at my house, but usually there's a text or something first, so I immediately jump to conclusions based around the worst possible scenario.

"Hey," I say, dropping onto the step beside her. My boots are dusty, there's dirt streaked up the legs of my jeans and I'm covered in grimy sweat from the mixture of exertion and arena dust. "Everything okay?"

She gives a stiff little nod but doesn't say anything. She hasn't even looked at me.

"Kait." I try again. "What's up? Did something happen with Connor?"

"What? No!" There's anger in her voice and she shakes her head violently, but at least she's looked up.

I don't say anything for a moment. I don't know what to say.

Something's not right. She's mad at me, but I can't think of anything I've done.

I feel sick, but not the good kind of sick I felt after Jonathan pressed his palm against my arm and told me I was amazing. My heart swoops thinking about it.

"Well, what is it then?" I say when I realise she has no intention of saying anything else.

"I'm … I'm trying to figure out why you've been lying to me." She finally looks directly at me. Her eyes are flinty. She's not messing around.

My stomach drops. There's no more heart swooping.

I don't know what she's talking about. I haven't lied to her. Unless … I try to speak, but no words come out and I end up opening and closing my mouth like a goldfish.

I take a few deep breaths, counting slowly like I've been taught. "What are you talking about?" I manage to gasp.

"Daniel." It's one word. A word I like, a person I adore, but her voice cuts me.

"I'm lying to you about Daniel?" I say, my heart sinking.

My stomach is churning again. Can a conversation make you throw up? I'm sure I haven't told her any lies about Daniel. I may have omitted a few things, but there were no lies.

"You keep telling me there's nothing going on."

"There isn't." I try to sound confident, but my voice is flimsy. Not at all convincing. "There is definitely nothing past friendship going on there."

Kaitlin pushes herself up off the step and spins to face me.

"You're going to keep lying to me? Why can't you tell me?

Were you with him on Saturday?" She crosses her arms across her chest and stares down at me.

I'm about to reply, to somehow explain what Saturday was without it sounding like a date, but she cuts me off.

"You don't even need to answer that because I know you were. Jess told me. She saw you two leaving Chester's together. She said he had his arm around you, and you still sit there and act like you're just friends?"

She uses air quotes around the "just friends" and I flinch at her voice. She sounds furious.

My eyes prickle and I know tears will be brimming any moment now.

I can't tell her the truth.

I don't know why.

It shouldn't be that big a deal, but it is.

The shame of it eats me up, and the thought of a relapse terrifies me.

Even now, when I have it mostly under control, the stupid wiring of my brain controls my life and I can't bring myself to confess it to her.

I never intended to keep it this big secret, but the longer I didn't tell her, the less it felt like I could.

It's not like I can say, "Oh, it's all over now." No, I'm going to be stuck like this pretty much forever, and no one else needs that burden.

"Kait," I say, with my voice shaking. I can't look at her, so instead study the aqua blue, strappy sandals she wears. "Dan and I *are* only friends. I promise. I'm really sorry, but I need to be somewhere. Can we talk later? I'll call you when I'm done."

She says nothing and eventually I peek up at her. She's glaring down at me.

"Whatever," she bites out. "Go enjoy your date or whatever with Daniel or whoever else you're seeing without telling me about." I flinch again at her words. "How would I know, since you don't tell me anything anymore?"

She turns and strides to her car parked at the curb, those strappy sandals tapping on the concrete footpath.

"Kaitlin!" I try to stop her before she goes, but I'm too stunned, too slow, and she's off, leaving me standing there at a complete loss.

***

The fog is back.

Sleep eluded me for much of the night and this morning I woke groggy and stiff. My head's clouded with cotton wool, my limbs heavy.

My alarm went off but I slept through it, along with my first backup one. Thankfully I woke up to my third and final alarm, but it meant I had to rush to get everything ready on time. There was no time for a run and barely time for a shower.

I pull into an empty parking spot and drag my feet towards school, head down to avoid eye contact and anyone who might try to make it with me.

Ugh, I cannot bear the thought of small talk.

I need Daniel.

Or Kaitlin.

Then I remember what happened yesterday afternoon. I shove those thoughts away before they claim my entire headspace.

Jonathan steals into my mind.

The image of him standing with Thea, leaning casually against the arena railing with the baby on his hip. The way the sun hit his dark hair, highlighting it with those touches of gold.

Then, when I'd helped him with the baby carrier and all I wanted to do was touch him and not stop.

The hint of exhaustion around his eyes as he talked of Thea's sleepless nights. His eyes were tired, but the deep green was as captivating as ever.

A strange pang of jealousy hits as I think of how he rested his hands against Thea's back.

I shove all thoughts of him away too. I'm not going there. It's hard enough inflicting myself on Dan.

And am I seriously jealous of a *baby* because he touched her? I shake my head. No way. No freaking way.

"Hey."

Someone falls into step beside me but it takes a moment to register. My brain is moving in slow motion.

I glance up for a moment and catch a glimpse of dark hair, a newly familiar and rather intoxicating jawline and the charcoal-grey jacket Jonathan favours.

It's as if I've conjured him.

"Oh, hey," I mumble, keeping my head down and watching our feet pacing along the concrete together. My hair falls over my face, forming a curtain between us, and I let it. I'm not ready to deal with anyone, let alone him. I don't know why, but my brain seems to short circuit every time I try to talk.

"You okay?" Jonathan touches his hand to my shoulder.

I flinch. I try to hide it, but I know I've done a bad job of it. His touch disappears.

"Yeah," I say, without looking up. "Just a bad night."

"I know that feeling," he sighs.

I peek up at him through my hair to see him rubbing his hand across his eyes, then dragging it through his hair.

"Thea not sleep again?" I can't help it. It's impossible not to be drawn into conversation with him.

He shakes his head and I catch the movement. I'm still reluctant to look up.

"Hollie."

This time his touch is by my wrist. The pressure is gentle, but it brings me to a halt and he turns me to face him. I'm captivated by his shoes.

"Are you sure everything is okay? You seem ... different today."

I know I need to look at him. I don't think he'll give up otherwise.

I drag my eyes away from the ground and look up, still avoiding his eyes. He's watching me closely and the green depths of his eyes – in which I could happily be lost forever – are searching my face.

"Yeah, I'm okay. I'm tired, but that's all. Really." I'm not sure I'm convincing, but I make myself meet his eyes.

He studies me for a moment, then after what seems like forever he apparently buys it. He gives a small nod and starts walking again.

"Okay, and nah, Thea does not like sleep." He sighs again, deeply this time. "Beth's exhausted but I don't know what to do to help. I think I've given her even more to worry about." He rubs at his hair again.

"I guess you help where you can, like yesterday," I say. "She likes having you here. I can tell. Plus, I can do some more to help out, too."

"Thanks, but you don't need to do more. It's amazing

everything you do already with the horses."

"Yes, but if there's anything else…" I trail off.

He smiles down at me. "I'll let you know. Thanks. It's nice to know you're around."

My face goes hot. Fabulous. Now to go with my puffy eyes, dark circles and flat hair, I've got a hot blush going on.

"And what you did last night was crazy impressive."

I shrug. I'm not that good. Harley is amazing and that makes my job easy – not that it feels like a job most of the time. I'm trying to help Beth get Harley all schooled up and sold. She took him on before she realised she was pregnant, so I'm doing what I can so she'll let me carry on riding. Without her, I have no idea what I'd do.

"Johnny!" A voice calls across the carpark, dragging out the name. Jonathan's head jerks up and he turns towards the sound.

It's Jake Daly.

Yay.

Jake's one of those guys who thinks he's absolutely hilarious, but he's really not at all, unless you enjoy making fun of people for nothing but your own amusement.

The thing with Jake though, is that I don't think he realises he's being cruel. He's a bit of an idiot, that's all. I sigh to myself as he jogs across the carpark to us.

"Hey, Jake," Jonathan – Johnny – says. "It's Jonathan, okay? Not Johnny."

Okay, so definitely not a nickname he appreciates.

"Jonathan. Sorry, man," Jake says, and slaps him on the back. He turns to me. "Hey, Hollie Dolly."

"Oh good God, no." I turn away, spotting Dan near the door to the English block. "See you later," I call to Jonathan as

I move away, striding with as much confidence as I can muster and hoping it looks better than it feels.

"Hey, lovely," Dan says as I approach. "How's New Guy?" He's got his troublesome smirk on and I wonder how much of the interaction he witnessed.

"God, Dan, I'm not in the mood," I mutter. "Jake called me Hollie Dolly."

Dan smirks harder, then bursts out laughing when he can't hold it anymore. He tries to quash it when I send a death stare his way, but ends up snorting before cracking up again.

"Hollie Dolly," he wheezes out between cackles.

"You ever say that again and you won't live to regret it," I say, but I can definitely feel the corner of my mouth trying to tug upwards.

Dan shakes his head. "I wouldn't bother repeating anything he says." He giggles a bit more. "No, he's too annoying." His laughter fades.

Dan and Jake have a history and as far as I know, it's not a pretty one. Dan doesn't really talk about it, but I'm pretty sure Jake made Dan's life a misery. He still tries to from time to time, being overly friendly and jovial, and trying to make Dan the butt of his jokes, but Dan doesn't buy into it anymore.

Apparently that's much less fun for Jake.

It also probably helps that while Jake is tall, he stayed weedy. Dan most definitely did not. Dan broadened across the shoulders and somehow developed a bit of an athlete's physique, not that he'd actually lower himself to doing sports.

"No," he says again. "But before Jake came over it looked like you and New Guy were getting friendly."

I sigh.

"Dan. I love you, but no. We're not doing this. I'm tired,

I'm having a really bad day. He wanted to know why I was being so cranky."

"Yeah, I'm not sure that's all it was," he murmurs as he gazes back across the carpark to where Jonathan and Jake are still talking.

I roll my eyes. "Believe me, that's all it was. Now come on, let's get to class."

CHAPTER 13

Hollie

I **PULL** into my usual parking spot at Beth's and turn off the car.

School dragged yet again. These days it just feels like something that prevents me from riding – and it keeps me around too many people.

I didn't see Kaitlin until lunchtime. She flicked a glare my way, then sat at the other end of the table, talking quietly with Connor. By the number of times they looked in my direction, I'm pretty certain they were talking about me.

I stabbed viciously at my fruit salad with my stupid plastic fork, but all that achieved was me spilling it all over the table. I cursed under my breath and began mopping up my mess.

"Day not getting any better, huh?"

I looked up to find Dan standing over me, like a light in the darkest tunnel.

He gestured and I shuffled over to make room for him on the bench seat. Perching on the end, he pulled something out of his pocket as he sat, then reverently placed it on the table in front of me.

A treat size packet of peanut M&Ms. My favourite. I gave the packet a poke.

"Rations, huh?"

He laughed, and I may have even smiled.

"Sorry. It was all I could get my hands on at short notice."

"Thanks," I said quietly, and my gaze automatically sought Kaitlin.

Of course, she'd seen the whole interaction.

Fabulous.

I sighed. My head had been throbbing most of the morning and I sat there thinking how I couldn't wait until the day was over. Or at least the school part.

Dan was a warm, solid comfort beside me, and despite the logical part of my brain telling me it was a very bad idea, I rested my head against his shoulder. In a not very polite manner, I told the logical part of my brain to leave.

But school finally ended, as always.

I glance up from my reverie to see Milo standing at the paddock fence waiting for me.

He's never shouted at me for something I haven't done.

I enjoy Tuesdays at Beth's because I only have to worry about training him. Harley and Alaska have Tuesdays off. Not that I ever begrudge riding them, but it's nice to have a slightly less hectic day.

"Hey, boy," I call to Milo as I climb out of my car. He stretches over the fence as I get closer and lips at my hair. "I missed you too."

I reach up and scratch between his ears. "Wanna go for a ride? I'll go get ready."

I grab my bag out of the car and head for the house, enjoying the crunch of gravel under my sneakers. I let myself in the back door, go through the laundry and slip into the bathroom.

The house is quiet and I hope that means Thea is giving Beth a break. Everyone's lack of sleep in this house is starting to worry me.

Jonathan doesn't seem to be home yet, but I thought that yesterday too.

Then he caught me dancing in the arena.

My face flames at the memory and the mortification pins me for a moment before I pull my t-shirt over my head and fling it to the ground. I'm focussing on horses only from here on out.

Five minutes later, I'm changed and headed for Milo.

I saddle him quickly and lead him to the gate heading out to the back paddocks. I'm aiming for a sneaky getaway.

I heard the low rumble of Jonathan's car while I was tacking up, but I'm still not feeling up to small talk.

As I'm settling onto Milo's back, Jonathan makes his way across the driveway, headed for the barn. I don't think he's seen me yet.

He's changed out of his school clothes, a collection of expensive-looking city clothes, and he's wearing worn jeans and an even more worn-out t-shirt with his now scuffed work boots. They were new at the weekend.

I stare at him as he crosses the yard. I can't figure the guy out.

What teenage boy gives up his life, his friends, family – everything – to move in with his aunt and her baby?

He changed schools mid-term, and he's working doing manual farm labour, which he's clearly unaccustomed to.

Judging by his clothes and car, I'm pretty sure he's not doing it for the money.

Then there's how most of the time he seems like a really nice guy, except for those flashes of anger.

And he's friends with Jake, but maybe that's only because Jake hasn't revealed his true self yet.

I shake my head, clearing the thoughts. None of it is my business and I have more than enough to deal with. I adjust my feet in the stirrups and collect the reins.

Jonathan spots me and waves.

"Hey, Hollie," he calls out.

I lift my hand in a wave then turn Milo away from the gate. Setting off across the paddock at a gentle trot, I try forcing my body to relax, which of course is impossible. You can't force relaxation; you need to let it come on its own.

A cloud of tension has been lingering across my shoulders and behind my eyes all day, but as I move with Milo's steady gait and feel the sun warming across my back it slowly begins to fade.

As we amble up and down hillsides and along farm tracks, and follow the highest ridgeline of Beth's property, my mind drifts. Like so many times recently, it wanders to Jonathan. My brain seems to like trying to puzzle him out.

At first glance he's like any other popular, confident guy strolling around school like he owns the place. He's good-looking, got a flashy car, a bunch of loud mates and not a care in the world.

Except I know that's not true.

I can't explain what makes me think that or what gives him away. It's only because I've seen him at home that I've noticed it. Maybe it was something Beth said – not that she really talks about him, except in passing about what he's doing on the farm.

But there's an unease in him. A sadness, maybe; a slip in his confidence. I'm not sure what it is exactly, but there's something, and I get the feeling it's something he doesn't want people to see.

I think back to Friday night, when I found him sitting in the gutter. It's not even that he got drunk and was sitting there – it was the total despair I sensed.

It's that, and it's how he's always telling me how he's an asshole, when really he's been anything but. It's like he's trying to behave like one to prove himself right.

I sigh, and Milo tosses his head.

The biggest problem of all is that I keep thinking about him. Even when I really don't want to be thinking about him.

The last thing I need, or can handle, is a crush on a self-confessed asshole, even if that's not really who he is.

Somehow, I'm convinced he's a good guy.

Regardless of my thoughts or feelings, he keeps swaggering around with his hair falling into his eyes.

And suddenly I'm thinking about his eyes again.

I'm a goner.

There are tiny pink baby clothes and miniature cot sheets still hanging on the washing line after I put Harley away on Thursday. We've done more flatwork schooling and had a quick ride up through the hills.

Wednesday was just another typical day. I went running, I

went to school, I didn't see Kaitlin at all. I came to Beth's and rode Alaska.

I thought of Jonathan too much, but didn't see him either.

Today, at least, I'm feeling more like the person I want to be.

I head over and start pulling the washing from the line.

It smells like sunshine; that fresh, clean smell you only get with line-dried laundry. I heft the basket onto my hip and kick my boots off at the side door.

Beth is in the kitchen, chopping vegetables. Thea is lying under a play gym thing on the floor, gurgling at the toys above her.

"Oh, Hollie," Beth says when she sees me, and moves to take the basket. "Thank you, but you really don't need to do that."

I pull the basket away and roll my eyes. "I know I don't need to, but I can and I will. I hear sleep's been in short supply around here." I head towards the stairs. "I'll put it in her room for you."

"You do too much, Hollie!" Her voice follows me down the hall.

Beth's house is an old country-style villa. It has wooden floors and probably no insulation, which means it's always slightly cold inside even on the hottest summer days, but it feels homey.

Compared to the stark modern lines of my own home, this feels like snuggling down in a cozy blanket and being wrapped in a hug all at once. I love it.

As an added bonus, thanks to Beth and Thea and now Jonathan, this house isn't filled with an eerie silence like home would be tonight, with Mum out at a work thing.

There's faint music coming from the kitchen radio and Thea's baby noises drift down the hall.

Being alone with my thoughts is a bad idea at the moment, especially after the fight – or whatever it was – with Kaitlin. I can't bring myself to confront her, and she doesn't seem to want to talk to me at all. The soft sounds of home life are soothing in the midst of all of that turmoil.

I make my way up the stairs. I haven't been up here since Jonathan moved in and I'm surprised he's taken the room at the top, directly across from the stairs. I don't know why, but I assumed he'd take the other spare room, down the far end of the house, where he could hide more easily.

His door is open as I reach the landing. He's sitting at a desk at the window, which I realise looks out over the arena. I can't hear music, but he's tapping his foot and nodding his head as if to a beat. He must have headphones in.

I pause for a moment and consider saying something. A warning that I'm lurking in his house again, perhaps. But we're in this awkward "Are we friends or are we not friends?" stage of knowing each other, and I don't know how much contact I should be initiating. Is it only a proximity thing? That I work where he lives?

Jonathan drops his head into his hands and lets out a groan.

I need to move.

I've been loitering here too long, and he doesn't need me watching whatever this moment is. Plus, at any moment he could turn around and find me standing awkwardly in his bedroom doorway.

I turn away and slink into the next room over, which belongs to Thea. Not that she ever sleeps in here. I place the basket on her change table and start folding her teeny onesies, or whatever they're called, and slip them into drawers as I go.

The familiar motions are soothing, like driving or riding. I try to focus on the task at hand; the soft cottons, the sweet smells, but my mind slips away, wandering from thought to thought. Every so often it pauses on Kaitlin, but I push it onwards. Somehow I have to deal with that, but right now isn't the time.

Before long my thoughts are lingering on the boy in the next room.

It doesn't take much for me to relive every moment we've touched, the tingling still present under my skin.

I can perfectly visualise the flash of green eyes under his scruffy fringe.

I wonder about him sitting in a gutter at a party.

And I wonder if we're friends.

CHAPTER 14

Jonathan

"HEY, BETH," I call. I can hear her moving about but can't pinpoint her location.

"Not Beth, sorry," a voice calls back from down the hall. I follow the sound and poke my head around the door of Thea's room.

Hollie is standing beside the dresser, a pile of tiny clothes in her hand. She slips them into the open drawer and pushes it closed with her hip. I catch my eyes following the movement of that hip and force myself to avert my gaze.

"Nope, definitely not Beth." I smile.

I haven't seen much of Hollie the last couple of days, not since Tuesday morning when she looked pale and tired. Her smile didn't come easily, and whatever was on her mind seemed to trail her for the rest of the day. I saw her at lunchtime sitting quietly with a group of friends. The dark-haired girl she was with last week sat at the opposite end of the table and as far as I can tell didn't speak to Hollie.

Hollie didn't speak to anyone until a tall guy with crazy curly blond hair joined her. It had to be Dan. They had a short conversation, then Hollie rested her head against his shoulder and stayed that way until the bell rang for afternoon classes.

I haven't seen her at school since, and barely at Beth's. She's waved hello but hasn't stopped to talk.

I'm drawing the conclusion she's probably – most likely – avoiding me.

But the tiredness has gone from around her eyes and she smiles back at me. So, maybe she wasn't avoiding me at all.

Or maybe she's simply happy from riding. Maybe it relaxes her, or distracts her, at least. I watched her from my bedroom window while trying to finish homework. She was a *very* good distraction from that, and I was highly disappointed when she finished and I had to concentrate on chemistry again.

"What are you doing?" I ask, leaning against the door frame.

She gives me a look, and fair enough. It was a fairly dense question.

"I'm folding washing," she says, holding up a pair of miniature pants with tiny pink frills around the bottoms of the legs.

"I can see that, but why?"

"Because I can. Because it helps Beth." She shrugs. "It's only a few minutes, but it's something else she doesn't have to worry about." She places the folded pants into a drawer and starts moving around the room, tidying things as she goes.

Guilt slices through my gut.

I'm supposed to be here helping Beth and yet here's this girl who owes Beth nothing, who is doing far more than she needs to.

Meanwhile, I've been sitting in my room retyping the same text message over and over, but never pressing send.

Yeah, so the chemistry homework didn't go that well.

I know Hollie offered to help, and I know she's happy to do it, but it doesn't feel right.

Or maybe I don't like the way it makes me feel because it highlights how unhelpful I've been.

This conversation suddenly doesn't feel easy anymore. The slice of guilt is widening, threatening to take me over completely as my brain throws up memories of all the ways I've failed everyone in my life.

Beth.

Kristen.

Luke.

Even Mum and Dad. I abandoned them too, in more ways than one. I went from being a normal, functioning human, who did all right at school, had an actual job, had friends but didn't cause too much trouble, to – in a flash – whatever it is that I am now.

Then, to top it all off, I heard a throwaway comment about Beth needing more help on the farm and I bailed on them completely, barely giving them a day's notice of my departure.

They let me go, of course. I suppose they thought it might help me. That the change of scenery might make me better, so I could be who I was before.

But they have no idea why I really had to leave: no idea what actually happened to Luke, and no idea that I have no clue how to make anything better, let alone myself.

The thoughts are spiralling, and as usual I don't know how to stop them.

My breath hitches.

My pulse races.

I'm inexplicably and suddenly hot and cold at the same time.

I press my hands against my eyes in a vain attempt to squash the images in my brain.

"Hey." There's a soft touch on my arm. It's there for a second before it disappears. I'm not sure if I imagined it. But there it is again. Firmer this time. A solid, warm weight on my bare forearm.

Hollie applies the tiniest amount of pressure and draws my hands away from my face. I can't look at her so I keep my gaze resting on her hand, still on my arm.

She's got bright pink nail polish on, but it's chipped and peeling. Heat is building in the place our skin touches, sending sparks up my arm.

It's a good feeling and I cling to it.

"Take a breath," Hollie says, voice quiet but firm.

I do.

It feels shaky, but I keep going, slowing my breath and my racing heart.

"I wanted to help out," she says, after I've managed to pull myself together a fraction. She drops her hand from my arm and it suddenly feels cold. "But if you don't want me in here I can stay outside and only handle the horses."

She goes to turn away.

I reach out for her, but I'm not sure if I should touch her. I'm not sure what I'd do if I felt her skin under my fingertips.

Right now, I'm not sure a simple touch to get her attention would be enough.

I wonder what it would feel like to trace the lines of her face. It's not the first time my thoughts have wandered this path.

I wonder if she'd close her eyes and let me.

I wonder what it would feel like to press my palms against her back, run them down her arms, pull her body against mine.

I'm not rational enough to deal with these thoughts right now.

I let my hand drop.

"That's not it," I manage. My voice is low and rough. "It's always nice to have you around."

She turns back to me and ducks her head, but not before I notice a hint of red in her cheeks.

Wishful thinking, I tell myself.

"I didn't mean to upset you again," she murmurs.

"You didn't."

And though she looks skeptical, it's the truth. She didn't upset me. I did that all by myself, by failing everyone and being a self-involved asshole.

"You must have a life that doesn't involve a baby's washing, though. I mean, that's why I'm here … to help Beth. Not that I'm doing a very good job of it."

I sigh.

"You'd be surprised at my complete lack of a life." She grins, and it does twisty things to my stomach. "Beth does so much for me, especially letting me ride. This is nothing. And my Mum is working tonight, so it's a few more minutes in a house that isn't weirdly silent." She steps closer to me again. "And you *are* helping. Simply having you here is helping Beth. She was so lonely before. Don't be so hard on yourself. I don't know a single teenage boy who'd think to fold baby washing."

She grins again and slips past me into the hallway, heading for the stairs with the washing basket swinging from her hand.

I stare at the now immaculate baby room for a moment before following her. I catch up with her at the bottom of the stairs.

"Dinner."

Wow. Smooth.

That was so indescribably uncool.

Hollie tilts her head and studies me. I clear my throat and expand on my invitation. "You could stay for dinner."

She smiles. "Thanks, but I can't."

"Why not? Beth won't mind. Unless you don't want to … which is okay." I'm getting even cooler with every word. I hold my breath, because I'm not sure I think it *is* okay if she doesn't want to stay.

Hollie shakes her head. "It's not that I don't want to …"

"What won't I mind?" Beth pokes her head out from the kitchen.

I'm not sure if she's going to save me or make this super-awkward conversation a billion times worse.

"Hollie staying for dinner," I blurt. I don't sound desperate at all.

"Oh, of course I don't mind," Beth says. "As long as your mum won't miss you."

"Her mum's working," I say. I raise an eyebrow at Hollie. It's a "See, there's no reason not to stay" eyebrow.

I'm more desperate for her to say yes than I realised.

She raises her hands in surrender. "All right, I'll stay." She turns to Beth. "As long as you're sure you don't mind."

"You know I don't. Plus, you make much better conversation than this guy." She grins. "I haven't figured out how to cook for two people and may have in fact made enough to feed an army, so you're really doing me a favour." Beth disappears back into the kitchen.

"That was unfair," Hollie says, turning to me. "Ganging up on me." She pouts, but I can see her smile fighting to get out.

"Sorry. If there's an actual reason you can't stay then…" I shrug. "But if you just didn't want to impose…" I lay heavy emphasis on the last word as I let it trail off.

"Maybe I didn't want to spend the evening with you?" But she says it with a smile. She turns for the kitchen. "You coming?"

I shake my head. "In a second. I have to finish something off upstairs."

Then, taking the steps two at a time, I go back to my phone that's sitting on my desk with a text message thread open, the reply section blank.

CHAPTER 15

Hollie

I SMOOTH my hair back into a fresh ponytail and study my reflection in the mirror over the hand basin.

I'm in Beth's downstairs bathroom, trying to clean myself up as much as I can for dinner. Retying my hair is about as good as it gets.

I considered changing back into my school clothes, which are shoved in the backseat of my car, but I've never changed out of my riding clothes the other times I've had dinner with Beth, so it seems a bit … *much*.

When I leave the bathroom there's a drum-heavy, twangy country song blasting from the kitchen. I'm surprised when I reach the doorway to see that Jonathan is there. After coercing me into staying for dinner he'd abruptly disappeared back upstairs to his room.

I'm even more surprised by the fact he's wearing the old cowboy hat that's always hung on the cluttered coat rack by the front door and *dancing*. I know country is most definitely Beth's style of music – I love it too – but I had not picked it for Jonathan's jam. At all.

I lean against the doorframe and watch as he executes a series of complicated steps across the room. He comes up behind Beth and spins her away from the bench where she's trying to prepare dinner. She twirls with him, then gives him a playful shove and turns back to the counter, giggling.

It's so good to see her laughing. She's been so exhausted lately that even her smiles are tired.

Jonathan notices me as he turns and dances his way over to me, a grin on his face.

It's nice to see him happy too – if the state of my stomach is anything to go by.

"Come join the party," he says, holding out a hand.

"I'm good right here, thanks," I say with a smile. I'm enjoying this far too much.

He looks damn good in his black t-shirt and dark jeans, his slightly too-long hair sticking out from under the brim of the hat. What is absolutely the best thing about this is that he's clearly putting on a show, so I can watch – and admire – without even feeling like a creeper.

"Aw, shucks now, darlin'," he says in a parody of Southern country charm. "You'll be a-breakin' ma heart." He pulls the hat off his head and clutches it to his chest.

"Your heart will be fine."

"Probably," he shrugs, his voice returning to normal. "But it'll be better if you join the party." Then he plonks the hat on my head, grabs my hand and pulls me into the kitchen, spinning me as he does.

I'm hoping he'll let me go … and also kind of hoping that he won't.

He doesn't, and insists on leading me through his own version of a line dance. Even Beth and Thea join in, the baby giggling and squealing as her mum scoops her out from under the play gym and spins her around the room.

Song after song blares through the little kitchen radio as we dance and laugh, and I feel the lightest I have in what seems like forever.

It's like the sensation I get when I'm riding, except this time there are other people involved.

Riding is a magical experience, but generally something I experience alone. I forget how much joy comes from being around other people.

Jonathan's hand is warm in mine and his other hand grazes against my side – a touch on the waist, pressure on my shoulder – as he guides me through the steps. Each brush sends sparks of electricity through my body.

My heart races and my breath is coming fast when he abruptly pulls me to him, our bodies flush for the briefest second, then dips me dramatically in time with the end of the song. He had to know it was coming and I'm surprised again that he'd know this music so well.

He holds me there for a moment, both of us staring into each other's eyes, his body leaning into mine.

My hand is resting against his bicep and I can feel the warmth coming from his skin through the fabric of his shirt. My pinky finger skims the edge of his t-shirt sleeve and the hot skin underneath.

He's so close to me I can see flecks of gold in his green eyes and the individual dark lashes fringing them.

I'm seeing everything at once in high definition.

And I have no idea where we are going to from here.

In a romance movie this is the time for an earth-shattering, life-changing kiss.

I, however, am fully aware I am not in a romance movie.

I'm also fully aware that life is already hard enough. It's hard enough having to take care of myself and deal with my own feelings and emotions. It's most definitely too hard to involve someone else. Especially someone who has so much of their own stuff going on.

The moment's lingering and it's like neither of us know what to do or how to get out of it. The music from the speaker has faded into an indistinct buzz.

All I can hear, see, feel, is Jonathan. His breath rasps in my ears, his face fills my vision – every little detail – and I can feel the heat of him, his heartbeat pulsing through his body.

Abruptly, a drum beat fills the room and it's not from the song currently playing on the radio.

Jonathan breaks out of whatever headspace he's been in while holding me and pulls me upright again. It's only been a few seconds but it feels like an eternity, and I'm both relieved and disappointed it's over.

Jonathan reaches into his back pocket and slowly pulls out his phone. He groans and tosses it, still ringing, onto the table.

Beth turns to eye him.

"That bad, huh?"

"It's Kris," he says with a small shrug.

"What's wrong with Kris? I thought you two were close?"

The memory of the phone call he received on Monday when I handed his phone to him comes back to me. The pretty girl who lit up the screen. Kristen.

"We are. I…" He pauses, shoving his fingers into his hair. "I don't want to talk to her right now," he says finally, a pained, tired look on his face. His buoyant mood is gone, evaporated in an instant.

The phone goes silent, then almost immediately rings again.

I'm standing watching this play out and realise I still have the ridiculous cowboy hat on my head. I pull it off, fiddling with the brim to give my hands something to do.

Beth squeezes Jonathan's shoulder and reaches for the phone. She answers the call and hits the speaker button.

I'm completely baffled. Who is Kris? Why would Jonathan not want to speak to her, but allow Beth to answer the call?

"Hey, Kris," Beth says towards the phone, sitting down at the table and gesturing for Jonathan to join her.

"BETH!" The voice squeals down the line.

"How are you?"

"I'm fabulous as always." A laugh. "But more importantly, how are you and Thea?"

She has the kind of voice that makes me think every sentence or question should be followed by sixteen exclamation marks.

I stop my brain. That was pretty bitchy. I'm pretty sure I'm jealous. It doesn't seem surprising to me that Jonathan would go for a girl who speaks with excessive punctuation. I feel like before he came here he was different. I'm not sure if it's a good or bad change, though.

"We're doing great. She's very fond of Jonathan." She smiles at him and I notice he hasn't moved, except to drag his hands through his hair several times more.

"Speaking of my brother dearest, where is Johnny and why won't he answer my calls?"

Hold up. *Brother*?

Huh.

The heavy feeling in my stomach abruptly disappears. So does the bitchiness.

Something else sneaks into my brain.

Johnny.

He let her call him Johnny, but was very firm with Jake that no one should call him that.

Interesting.

"I'm right here," Jonathan says, his voice cracking a little as he drops onto the bench opposite Beth and shoves his hands back into his hair. A nervous habit, for sure. "I'm not not answering your calls. I talk to you all the time." He's trying to be exasperated, but the smile breaks through. "It's not my fault you have no life and have to ring me constantly for your only source of enjoyment."

"Ooh, ouch!" Kris laughs again. "What ya doing?"

"Country music dance party," Beth replies instantly.

Jonathan groans. "Geez, Beth, thanks for ruining my cred."

"It's your sister," Beth bites back, but with a cheeky grin. "You never had any cred."

More laughing bursts down the line.

"This is true. But seriously, the country music again? How're you gonna get a girl with that?"

I'm still standing awkwardly to the side of the kitchen, watching this conversation play out, and at her comment my skin flares with heat.

"Ha. Ha," Jonathan deadpans. "The joke's old, Kris. We all know you love country too, only you refuse to admit it."

"Besides, he'd do all right, wouldn't he, Hollie? Country music or not." Beth turns to me and my face flares so hot I worry it might melt off. Do I actually have to answer that?

"WHO IS HOLLIE?" The pitch of Kris's voice could shatter windows.

"Woah, Kris. Settle down," Jonathan laughs, but his face is looking a little flushed too. I tell the inner monologue that notices it to shut the hell up, and will my heartbeat to settle.

"Hollie works for me, with the horses," Beth explains. "She's riding them all for me while I can't."

"Is this whose car you left your phone in?"

"Yes, that one. And she's right here, so be nice." Jonathan sounds grim, like he doesn't want to introduce me to his sister.

"Ooooh, hi Hollie!"

"Um, hi." I edge towards the table and Beth gestures me towards her seat as she gets up.

"I'm finishing dinner Kris, but we'll catch up properly soon, yeah? You need to come and meet your cousin."

"I'm working on it," Kris chirps in her sparkly little voice. Part of me wants to dislike her purely for her perkiness, but I can't. "Bye Beth, kiss Thea a thousand times for me."

I slip into Beth's vacant seat, setting the hat on the table beside me, not quite sure what to expect from this conversation.

"So, Hollie, what's the goss on my big brother?"

"Umm…" I hesitate. "There isn't any. I don't think." I take a moment, wondering if there's anything I actually know about him.

Jonathan is watching me from across the table, one eyebrow raised. My heart jerks at the hint of humour in his gaze, the upward tilt of the corners of his mouth. "Nope," I say finally, "I know nothing."

"Is he like, silently threatening you or something?"

I laugh, hard. "I think your brother is one of the least threatening people I've ever met."

At this Jonathan raises a second eyebrow, looking genuinely shocked. I don't know how to process that, so I glance away, fingertips finding the brim of the hat again. "Also, I'm not the person to go to for gossip."

"You're quite right. He's a giant teddy bear, isn't he?" she teases.

"God, Kris, shut up," Jonathan butts in. "Did you call for a reason or just to drag me?"

"A reason, of course … as if dragging you wasn't a valid reason on its own. You didn't let me tell you about Luke the other day."

I'm looking down at the phone when she says this, but Jonathan jerks so violently my gaze is drawn directly to him.

The easy lines of his posture and the laughter in his features are gone. His face is white, his jaw and shoulders rigid with tension. His hand lies on the table next to the phone and it twitches ferociously, like he wants to pick up the phone and hurl it across the room.

I thought the phone call from Kris had affected him, but the mention of Luke – whoever he is – has taken it to a whole other level.

"He came home on Monday," Kris carries on, oblivious to the turmoil she's caused in her brother. "He's doing so well."

"That's … that's awesome," Jonathan manages to croak. "It's happened quickly."

"Yeah, it has, but like I said, he's doing well."

Jonathan's hand is tapping out a silent rhythm, full of tension. Beth is moving around the kitchen behind me, finishing off dinner. I'm not sure she's even realised what's going on.

"He misses you, though," Kris says softly.

"Yeah, well. I'm sorry about that. But there isn't much I can do." He grabs the phone. "Look Kris, I gotta go. I'm sorry. Dinner. I'll talk to you later, okay? Say hi to Mum and Dad."

Before she even has the chance to respond he ends the call.

He clasps the phone between his hands, knocking it lightly on the table, his eyes cast down.

I'm left sitting here staring at him, with no idea whatsoever what just happened.

The mere mention of this guy Luke and Jonathan completely flipped.

He looks like he desperately needs a hug, but I'm not sure we have that kind of friendship, and even if we do I'm not sure he'd welcome it right now.

The tension is radiating from him, but it's not anger this time.

It's pain.

Hurt.

My mind flashes back to the photo I spotted on the laundry windowsill last weekend, the morning after the party. It was a picture of Jonathan and another guy, grinning like fools.

I don't know how, but I know the other guy in the photo is Luke.

Jonathan still hasn't moved except for the small repetitive taps of the phone against the table. He hasn't looked up from where his gaze is locked on the tabletop.

I reach across the table and brush my fingertips across his knuckles. His hands freeze and he slowly raises his head to look at me.

"You okay?" I whisper, aware Beth is behind us, but still oblivious to what's happened.

He gives a jerky little nod, changes it to a shake, then gives up and shrugs.

"Don't want to talk about it," he mutters, barely audible. Then at a normal volume he adds, "Need any help, Beth?" Somehow he's managed to quell the tremor in his voice.

"I'm all good," she calls over her shoulder. "It'll be a couple more minutes."

My hand is still lying stretched across the table, next to Jonathan's. Without pausing to think about it or to consider and carefully weigh the pros and cons, I grab his hand and briefly squeeze it before letting go. I stand up and turn away to give him some space to gather himself.

Thea is hanging out in her bouncer in the corner and I lift her from it. She's soft and warm and coos at me with her sticky little smile.

The only thing better than a cuddle with a baby is a cuddle with a horse, and I can't fit one of them in the kitchen, so I hand Thea to a dumbstruck Jonathan and help Beth carry plates to the table.

CHAPTER 16

Jonathan

BY THE TIME the sound of Hollie's car fades into the night, I'm sprawled on my bed in the dark.

It's easier in the dark.

Turning on the light means allowing it into the murkiest little crevasses of my brain that I prefer to keep sealed and locked away.

The problem is, even lying here in the dark, those sealed up crevasses have been cracked open, split wide, like every time I'm confronted with, and reminded of, the full extent of what I've done.

Luke.

My best friend.

The image of him lying in a hospital bed battered and broken flickers across my mind. Tears streaking his face, drying in their tracks as the doctors explain his injury.

The crushed vertebrae, the potential spinal cord damage, the chance of him not being able to walk again.

My best friend, who was larger than life, who filled a room

with his presence, who was always grinning and laughing and up for an adventure.

The one who could have been a mountain bike champion, or a professional drummer.

He lay in that hospital bed, shocked and silent, staring out the window and refusing to even acknowledge the conversation.

I stood in the corner of the room and watched as he tried to swipe the tears off his face but flinched instead as he touched the bruise on his cheek. He tried to hide it from me, but he couldn't, even if he refused to look at me. I knew him too well.

I willed him to glance my way, to acknowledge me. But he never did.

His parents asked question after question of the doctors, most of which couldn't be answered. It was all a matter of time, they said.

The biggest question though, the one they were desperate for an answer to, wasn't for the doctors. Their question was for Luke, and he refused to answer.

I knew the answer.

I could have told them.

But I wouldn't.

I couldn't.

I knew exactly what happened.

I knew why it happened.

I knew, because it was entirely my fault.

CHAPTER 17

Hollie

IS seventeen too young for a heart attack?

Probably.

It's racing though – my heart – and I'm considering my options for the nearest place I can vomit. Would I make it to a bathroom or should I aim for the trees across the carpark?

I'm standing beside Jonathan's car. It's immediately after the final bell and I raced here to catch up with him before he left.

And now I'm waiting, and second-guessing myself every moment.

I take a deep breath and lean against the side of the bonnet like I saw him do the other day, feigning confidence.

I look around, scanning the swarm of students, but can't see his dark hair among them.

He's got to be here somewhere. I saw him earlier, albeit briefly. I spotted him between classes and tried to call out, but he was gone before I even got his name out.

I stand abruptly, taking a few steps away from the car.

Maybe he doesn't want to talk to me.

Maybe he saw me this morning and headed in the other direction on purpose.

Deep breath.

Whatever happened last night, whatever upset Jonathan and made him withdraw into himself, has nothing to do with me.

I'm almost sure of it.

He was fine until that phone call. He was happy, he was having fun. After the call he tried to come back from it, but he struggled.

Maybe it *was* me.

No.

It was something to do with the guy his sister had mentioned.

Luke.

Maybe he was the guy from the picture.

He has to be the guy from the picture.

I think back, trying to recall the details of the photo. I'd tried not to, but curiosity got the better of me and I'd found myself studying it.

I am fully aware of how gorgeous Jonathan is.

I can no longer deny it, especially after last night. The way his body moved and the way it moved with mine, the heat building between us.

The movement of his hips, the cut of his jeans and the way his t-shirt sleeve curved across his bicep were undeniably hot.

When his face breaks into that slightly crooked smile or he raises an eyebrow in a sardonic question, he's utterly gorgeous.

And Luke – if that's who's in the picture with him – he's definitely hot too, with long black hair and grey eyes crinkled in the corners as they laugh together.

Jonathan looks different in that picture, though. His hair is shorter, like he actually cares what it looks like, and the grin on his face is like none I've ever seen from him. There's an energy in him that is missing now. Even dancing last night in his aunt's kitchen, laughing as he twirled us around the room, it was missing.

Then it hits me, and I stop my pacing mid-step.

Were Luke and Jonathan a couple? Maybe it's heartbreak that brought him here.

But then what did Kris mean about Luke coming home? And why would she bring him up if he was Jonathan's ex? Unless of course she doesn't know. Maybe he isn't out yet.

I scratch at a fingernail, scraping off a bit more of the chipped polish. I don't know why I even bother with it. It lasts about five minutes around the horses. I look at it in disgust and sigh.

I don't know why I'm waiting here. If Jonathan wanted me to know what was going on he'd tell me. And if he doesn't want me to know, then it's none of my business.

"Hey, Hollie." His voice snaps me out of my internal debate.

I turn to face him but can't make any words leave my mouth. I wave a hand in the air, trying to gesticulate my meaning. I fail.

"Everything okay?" he asks.

He's hesitant. I know he is.

He's trying for his usual easy confidence but it's not quite there, and for some reason I can see through the cracks. He's trying desperately to hold it together.

He looks even more exhausted than usual today. I wonder if Thea kept him awake, or if it was his own demons.

"I was here to ask you that." The words leave me in a rush, one big exhale.

He studies me, then – a beat too late – replies. "Yeah, of course. Why wouldn't I be?"

I shrug. "Er, no real reason … umm … last night." Oh, I'm so awkward. The urge to vomit washes over me again.

He sighs quietly and leans against the car, where I was moments ago. I smile a tiny bit when he runs his hand through his hair. I could have predicted it.

"What?" he asks, his expression guarded.

I shake my head, fighting against the tugging that wants to turn my lips into a smile.

"Tell me." He sighs heavily.

I can't not tell him. I lean against the car and realise immediately that I'm far, far too close to him. But to move now is too awkward.

I can feel the heat coming off him as our shoulders brush.

"It's that thing you do with your hair," I mutter, heat flaring across my cheeks.

He glances at me, then at his hand. "Do I do it a lot?"

"Only when frustrated, angry, upset, happy, laughing, making a bad joke or if your hair is in your eyes."

He laughs, and there's a flash of his usual happy self. When it subsides he looks a little less tense.

I smile at him sideways, peeking out from beneath my own hair. He shifts his weight and his thigh touches mine, denim against denim. A flame curls in my belly.

His fingertips brush my temple and I twitch. I was so distracted by his knee that I didn't notice him lift his hand. He freezes like a wild animal caught in headlights.

Our eyes meet and I somehow manage to hold his gaze,

both willing him to continue and thinking that this is a completely terrible idea.

A moment passes, then he continues his movement, brushing the hair back from my eyes and sliding it behind my ear. Goosebumps ripple down my arm.

"You should do it yourself sometimes," he murmurs, deep green eyes holding mine. His fingertips are still warm against my scalp and I feel my breath catch.

I don't know who moves, but we're suddenly very close. Closer than last night. I can see each eyelash, the darker ring of green around his iris.

Movement makes my eyes flick to his mouth. He's caught his bottom lip between his teeth. I'm pretty sure he's about to kiss me – and if he isn't, then I'm going to kiss him.

I'm extremely aware of my body angled towards his, touching along our thighs. My hand has made its way to rest against the car bonnet, right beside his hip. My knuckles brush the denim of his jeans.

His hand slides down and brushes against my neck.

Tingles spread along my skin and another wave of goose-bumps springs up on my arms. I'm hot and cold all at once.

He moves a fraction closer.

This is actually happening.

My stomach flips.

"Hollie!"

I pull away from Jonathan, my heart racing and cheeks flaming.

"Oh, God. Fuck. Sorry." Dan stands in front of us, both hands covering his mouth. What I can see of his face is horror-struck.

Jonathan's shoved himself away from me. His hand finds its way to his hair and tangles itself in it.

"Man, shit," he says. "Look man, fuck, I'm sorry. I wasn't hitting on your girlfriend. Except God, I think I really was. I'm sorry. *Fuck*." He slams his hand against the bonnet and I jerk away in shock.

Dan stares at us for a moment, the look of horror shifting to one of confusion, then he cracks up laughing; that loud, boisterous laugh I usually love.

Jonathan glances at me then back to Daniel, hand still tangled in his hair.

"I didn't mean to," he mutters while Dan stands there wheezing, trying to control himself.

I reach out my foot and kick him in the shin.

"Dude," Dan finally says as his laughter subsides, "Dude, stop looking like I'm gonna hit you or something. I love Hollie, but she's not my girlfriend." He says the last word like it's something hilariously disgusting and follows it up with a little shudder to drive the point home. I smack him on the arm. He has the decency to look a little bashful. "I'm sorry for interrupting, er, whatever was going on over here. I'm Daniel, by the way." He holds out a hand to Jonathan, who takes it suspiciously.

"Jonathan."

"Nice to meet you. We should catch up later. You're coming to the party, right?"

"Uh…" Jonathan's gaze flicks to me, then back to Dan.

"Come with Hollie. It's at my place." Dan turns to me. "Holls, I need your car." He holds out his hand and I stare at him, my mind struggling to keep up. It's still tangled in the whole Jonathan-was-about-to-kiss-me situation. Dan flexes his fingers in the universal "hand them over" gesture and I auto-matically reach for my keys, then pause.

"And how am I going to get to Beth's? And home? Then back to yours?"

He waves his hand in the air, gesturing enthusiastically towards Jonathan and his car.

"Come on," he pleads. "I may have forgotten to pick up the glasses yesterday, I didn't drive today and Mum will kill me if we have a party with no glasses."

Jonathan is watching us as if we've completely lost all reason, and to be fair I don't blame him.

Dan's my best friend and I love him dearly, but sometimes even I struggle to keep up with him.

Does he not notice the tidal waves of awkwardness rolling between me and Jonathan? Does he not realise he interrupted us almost kissing and now he expects us to get in a car together like it never happened?

And all this time Jonathan thought Dan was my boyfriend. Clearing that up will be a fun conversation.

What I do know is that Dan forgetting to do something for someone is a big deal. He never forgets something he's said he'll do. He never lets anyone down or breaks a promise.

I can tell by the strain in his face that it's a huge thing for him to forget. And he's right, a party with nothing to drink out of seems incomplete.

I turn to Jonathan. "Would that be okay?" I hate the way my voice comes out when I have to ask someone for something, even something as simple as a ride. It's all soft and wavering and pathetic.

Jonathan takes a moment, then nods. "Yeah, I can give you a ride. I owe you a couple anyway. Come on." He turns away, slipping into the driver's seat and tossing his backpack into the backseat.

"I'm going to kill you for this," I grumble to Dan as I fish my keys out of my pocket and hand them over. He smooshes me into a hug.

"Sure thing. Right after you thank me." He ruffles my hair, kisses his fingertips and presses them to my cheek.

"Don't go there," I warn.

He grins, but I can see the relief in his eyes. "Thanks for this, Hollie. Honestly." He holds up the keys as I scurry around to the passenger side of Jonathan's car.

As I'm sliding into my seat I hear Dan's voice. "Be good, you two."

I slam the door as Jonathan turns the key.

CHAPTER 18

Jonathan

HE'S NOT HER BOYFRIEND.

Not her boyfriend.

Not.

Boyfriend.

The words are tumbling around in my head. Over and over they go.

As soon as Hollie is in her seat I swing my car out of its parking space, and I'm on the road before she has her seatbelt on.

It's a dick move. I'm fully aware of it. But I need to get away from that situation, and fast. Except, I brought Hollie with me and my brain feels like it's malfunctioning.

Firstly, that guy isn't her boyfriend.

I mean sure, I've never seen them all over each other like the couples at my old school, but I kind of assumed Hollie was a quiet person and didn't want that kind of PDA-inducing attention.

I've seen them a few times when he had his arm draped around her shoulder and I know I've seen them hugging.

Then there was the other day when she spent most of lunchtime with her head resting against his shoulder.

There was the date, and him calling her gorgeous. Her being gorgeous is definitely a statement of fact, but I'm not aware of many guys who go around saying it to girls they aren't dating.

Plus she told me she was in love with him. That they were a couple.

I'm sure of it.

Definitely about the loving him bit.

He's admitted he loves her. Obviously he doesn't mean it like that.

It's like trying to do a jigsaw when the pieces don't match and half of them aren't even part of the puzzle.

Add to that the flashes of what happened last night and right before Daniel interrupted us. The feel of Hollie's body under my hands, both firm and soft, the heat from her skin and the way it reddened or got goosebumps – or both – when I touched her.

I spent the day trying to distract myself from thoughts of Luke by thinking about Hollie. Distraction or torture? I'm not exactly sure. But every time Luke sneaked into my brain I pushed him out and filled the space with Hollie. It was a dangerous game.

They were nice thoughts – bloody amazing ones, actually – but reminding myself I can't get close, that I don't deserve to be close to her, was a cold chill. And sometimes, even thinking about her blonde hair slipping from her ponytail, or the way her eyes spark when she laughs, wasn't enough to keep away the Luke-shaped demons.

I hate that I left. Hate that I abandoned him.

But it was pretty clear that he couldn't stand to be around me anymore, not after what I'd done. So I solved the problem for him.

I left so he could focus on getting better.

So he didn't have to be constantly reminded what an asshole his best friend was.

Similar thoughts were swirling around in my head when I approached my car and saw Hollie there, waiting for me.

All reason was gone. The mental struggles and debates had left me exhausted.

Surely leaving Luke behind and letting him put his life back together without me was penance enough. Would he begrudge me this small respite in the form of a pretty girl with a warm smile and excessive kindness?

I was apprehensive approaching Hollie, but I couldn't avoid her.

I needed to get to my car.

She surprised me though, by making me laugh, and before I knew it we'd slipped into the easy conversation we always seem to have.

Then we moved past the conversation. Way past it.

All I've been able to think about was how it would feel to touch my lips to hers.

We were both hesitant, but at the same time she moved closer, pressed her leg against mine. I felt her fingers brush against my hip right before Daniel called out to her and she jerked away.

Or I jerked away.

Because I realised what I was doing – what I'd almost done.

My mind was all tangled up in thoughts of Luke, and Hollie's relationship with Daniel was the furthest thing from it

… until he caught me almost making out with his girlfriend in the parking lot.

Except, she's not actually his girlfriend.

I exhale slowly and try to relax my knuckles on the steering wheel. They're white and starting to ache with tension. My gear changes are harsh and my poor gearbox is getting a hammering.

I glance over at Hollie. It's the first time I've been able to look at her.

She's sitting there in the passenger seat, hunched forward with her hands clasped around her knees. Her head is down and facing away from me, so she's either staring at the door or out the window, watching the businesses around school turn to suburbs. Eventually those will turn to paddocks as we near Beth's place.

Hollie's hair is out today and it's fallen back down to hide her face from me. My fingers itch and I desperately want to reach out and push it back, like I did only a few minutes ago. Those few minutes feel like an eternity already.

My mouth is dry, but I'm determined to speak. I don't know what to say though, so I open my mouth and hope for the best.

"Is this all some kind of elaborate joke?" My voice is rough.

"What? No!" I see her body jerk in my peripheral vision.

"You told me he was your boyfriend." My voice wavers a little on the word boyfriend.

Smooth. So smooth.

I'm watching the road, but I flick quick glances Hollie's way to gauge her reaction. I don't know if I'm mad or sad that she misled me.

God, I have no idea what's going on, or how to handle anything anymore – if I ever did.

"No I didn't," she says, her voice quiet. "I guess I maybe let you assume he was. But no, he's not. He never has and he never will be." She hasn't turned away from the window yet.

"Why?" Oh, apparently I'm angry about it.

She finally looks over at me, gives a small shrug when I glance her way and goes back to the window.

"Why did you let me assume? And what was that before? Are you trying to make me be a jerk?"

She flinches at my words and I don't blame her. I really am the asshole I warned her about the night we met.

She turns slowly to face me, her eyes blazing. At least she's not going to let me be nasty without a fight. "You think I tried to … what? Seduce you? To prove you're an asshole? Ever considered you're bloody good at being one all on your own without my help?"

She's fully facing me now, and I'm glad I have to focus on the road so I have an excuse not to look her directly in the face. Her look could kill.

She's so goddamn fucking gorgeous, and also absolutely one of the nicest people I've ever met, so…

"No," I say quietly, the rage from a moment before sliding away. "I don't think that." I shove my hand into my hair and feel my lip twitch like it's trying to smile, thinking about her calling me out on my annoying habit. "I'm sorry." She nods, and I continue. "You're right about the hair thing, though. I can't fucking stop."

Her icy glare cracks and a tiny laugh escapes. I smile back at her, glad the tension has broken.

"I didn't deliberately mislead you," she says. "But you did

sort of assume, and I guess it was easier to have you think I was with Dan. I figured it would stop things getting weird between us. Like the whole "does he like me, do I like him", if both answers are yes, is anyone actually going to do anything about it, or are we going to be weird and awkward. And even if both answers are yes, do I even want that because … I'm really not sure I can at the moment." Her words tumble out in a jagged, jumbled stream.

She wrings her hands in her lap and I notice her body is angled away from me again, hunched in the corner. I reach over and catch her hand, giving it a little squeeze before laying it softly back in her lap and letting go.

"I get it. It was easier for me to think there wasn't even a possibility you'd be interested. Until, well, suddenly it wasn't easier anymore." I study the road intensely. "We'd have moments, or what I thought were moments, and then I'd remember Daniel and hate myself. But honestly, your apparently imaginary boyfriend was the last thing from my mind back there … until he showed up, anyway."

I glance at her again. Her cheeks are pink. I want to brush my fingers along them, to feel the heat there. But I grip the steering wheel tighter and turn into Beth's driveway.

As soon as I stop the car Hollie is out the door and off across the yard. So much for the conversation I thought we were having.

Then I notice Beth is in the yard, Thea tucked into the carrier and Harley trailing her around the perimeter.

Harley stops and jerks at the lead rope and his legs start to buckle underneath him. Hollie grabs the lead from Beth and urges the little horse forward, her movements tense.

I climb out of the car and make my way towards them,

confused as hell. It looks like Harley wants to lie down. What's so wrong with that?

"What's going on?" I ask as I approach. Beth turns to me. Her face is pale, accentuating the dark circles under her eyes.

She's utterly exhausted. Thea is fussing and grizzling.

"Harley's colicking. We need to keep him walking. If he lies down he could twist his gut."

"That's not good?" I ask, already knowing the answer.

Beth shakes her head, swaying a little.

"Does Hollie know what to do?"

Beth nods this time, and sways again. "Yeah, she does. I need to call the vet, but I haven't got my phone on me and every time I let him stop he tries to lie down."

"Go inside, call the vet and have a rest. If Hollie can tell me what to do, I'll help her take care of him."

Beth opens her mouth and I know a protest is coming. She presses her hand against her forehead.

"Aunt Beth," I say, gently pulling her hand down. "Let us help. It's why we're here. Go and look after yourself and Thea. If we need you, one of us will come and get you."

She sighs, then leans into me as I wrap my arms around her. I'm not much of a hugger, but I've never seen someone more in need of one. She presses her face into my shoulder for a moment and I suddenly understand the magic of hugging.

"All right. I'll call the vet," she says, pulling away.

"And then rest."

"Thank you." She squeezes my arm and heads for the house.

I turn back to Hollie who is still walking around the yard, encouraging Harley to follow her.

"What do you need me to do?" I ask, falling into step beside her.

She shrugs. "Not much right now. He needs to keep walking. Where's Beth?"

"Gone to ring the vet, then she'd better be putting herself and Thea down for a nap."

"Good." She gives me a tight smile. "Until the vet's here I need to keep him moving. I can take care of it if you've got other things to do."

I nod. "I've got a few things to do out here, so I'll be right nearby if you need something. I'll go check Beth's doing as she's told and I'll be right back."

CHAPTER 19

Hollie

HARLEY IS GOING to be fine.

The vet arrived half an hour after Beth made the call. Jonathan took over walking Harley, giving me time to rush through the necessities of caring for the other horses.

By the time I ran back from checking on Milo and Alaska, the vet was pulling up beside the yard gate. She poured something down Harley's throat and the colic settled fairly quickly after that.

I offered to stay with Beth in case she or Harley needed me again, but Jonathan insisted I go to the party and said he'd stay.

"Party?" Beth perked up at the word.

Jonathan grimaced.

"Yeah, Dan's," I said.

"You're definitely going, Hollie." She turned to Jonathan. "Are you invited?"

He looked sullen, but grudgingly agreed.

"Then you're going too. It's good for you to get out and

meet some new people. Hollie has nice friends. Be friends with them."

"Plus," I put in, "I can't go without you. You're my ride, remember?"

He looked me over, eyes roving from head to feet. His lips hitched into a lopsided smirk. "True. But I'm not taking you anywhere looking like that." He tossed his keys to me. "Go get ready and come back for me, yeah?"

So here I find myself, driving Jonathan's car back to Beth's place after getting ready. This machine is in immaculate condition. He clearly loves it. I can't believe he was so cavalier handing over the keys.

I rushed home, showered and threw on the first outfit that came to mind. I put on basic makeup and wished I had more time to do it properly, but it's a fine line between looking good and taking forever.

I wish I'd been able to get ready with Kaitlin, blasting out cheesy pop songs and singing along at the top of our voices while debating outfit choices and makeup looks. She always makes me feel more confident in my decisions.

Except, somehow, we still aren't talking.

I can't shift the memory of Monday afternoon from my mind.

I can't forget the way she accused me of lying.

And I did lie. Not to be cruel to her, but I guess to protect myself. Unfortunately I still don't know how to unravel the mess I've found myself in.

She doesn't want to talk to me. I don't know how to start a conversation with her so we can move past what she said and what I've done.

I miss her so badly. Not only over these last few days, but for the several months before too.

As the darkness of depression crowded in, I pulled away from her.

She started going out with Connor and I sank lower and lower.

I was jealous, I know it. And now, all these months later, and after what happened on Monday, I don't know how to cross the divide between us.

Maybe turning up with Jonathan will help. Maybe it'll give her a reason to come and talk to me. She's nothing if not curious. Or maybe she'll assume I'm dating both Dan and Jonathan.

Geez.

Then there's Jonathan himself I have to worry about.

He thought I was dating Dan, too.

But now he knows I'm not, and we so obviously nearly kissed in the carpark. There's no way I can continue denying the feelings that stir in me whenever I see him. Heck, whenever I think about him.

But now we're at that awkward, weird place I've been trying to avoid.

I don't even know if he actually likes me or was simply struck by an urge to kiss me. I think he said he did like me, but the drama with Harley ended our conversation prematurely.

I suppose I have to deal with the rest of that conversation at some point.

I pull up in front of the house. My shoes clunk noisily on the timber decking as I climb the steps and I wince. I always feel a little awkward in heels, and the noise they make exacerbates that awkwardness.

Jonathan meets me at the door.

His gaze flickers over me, taking in my navy skirt and the dark pink satin top.

It's like he's trying to look me in the face but can't quite manage it. My cheeks feel warm – again – under his gaze. I shift and he smiles at me, thankfully looking me in the eye as he does.

Not that I can judge, because I am definitely looking at him.

He's in simple jeans and a t-shirt, and he's wearing this dark blue casual jacket over the top, but there's something about it – or about him – that's giving me butterflies.

"Ready to go?" he asks, stepping out and pulling the door shut behind him.

"You need to change," I say, raising my hand to stop him in his tracks. My fingers brush the front of his jacket and the tips feel like they're on fire.

"Change?" He looks down at himself.

"Yeah. I'm sorry. I should have said, it's a bit fancier than t-shirts." I gesture to myself, trying to somehow wordlessly explain the dress code based on my own outfit.

"Button down shirt?"

I nod. "Your jeans will be fine, but a proper shirt would go down well."

He nods and heads back inside. "Be right back."

He really is right back. Which is great, because I was starting to freak out that I'd abruptly told a guy I liked, but really didn't know that well, how to dress, and it was a little weird. He's still buttoning his shirt as he comes down the stairs, jacket now tossed over his arm.

"Is tucking it in compulsory?" He gives me a dark look. I

shake my head and he brightens again, then starts rolling the sleeves. This time I let him leave the house.

"Beth all okay? Harley's okay?"

Jonathan nods and moves towards the car, shrugging into his jacket.

"Yep. She's gone to bed already with an alarm set for an hour to check on Harley." He shakes his head. "I told her I'd check on him when I got home but it's not enough apparently, even for an exhausted mother."

I laugh. "That's Beth for you."

"I know. I have no idea how she manages to do it all."

"Me neither," I say, slipping into the passenger seat again. All this driving around together is starting to get comfortable.

"So," Jonathan says, starting the engine, "What can you tell me about this party I've been roped into going to? Who'll be there? Is there a specific reason for it? Why do I need to be wearing a dress shirt? Etcetera."

"Okay, so Dan's parents host this annual party." I pause for a moment, thinking over the various rumours surrounding the party and wondering which I should tell him first. "Rumour has it, it's to celebrate the birthday of Dan's mum's great aunt Kelsey, who left them the house. She died about fifteen years ago, but they celebrate her every year with this big party."

"Okaaaaay." Jonathan drags out the word, clearly wondering what he's got himself into.

"The real reason, though, is that when Natalie – Dan's mum – was setting up her event planning business, she threw a big party to showcase her talents. It went off, and she carried it on every year. Now it's really just an excuse to throw a party, but she sometimes has clients and staff and other important people there, so we have to behave and wear sensible shirts.

144

Dan's family hosts a bunch of different parties every year, I think mostly because they find them awfully fun."

"You sound like you don't find them awfully fun?"

"Ah, sometimes. They're not really my thing, but this one's a lesser evil because it's 'classy'." I give him a look that hopefully conveys I don't get the whole teenagers-drinking-to-excess-and-grinding-on-each-other scene.

"Ah yes, dress shirts do make things classy." He smirks. "I haven't known you long and this is the second party you've gone to – that I know of – so they can't be all bad."

I smile. I can't help myself around him.

"No, they're not all bad. Sometimes I even have a good time, but I don't like big, noisy crowds, or drinking, or how people behave when they're drinking…" I trail off.

"Yeah, sorry about that." He glances over and gives me a sheepish little smile.

"I wasn't actually meaning you," I say, "but yeah, I suppose it's similar."

"So why go if they aren't really your thing?"

"Because I'm a sucker." I sigh and lean against the door. "Kaitlin begged me to go to the last one, and this is Dan's, so here I am."

"Kaitlin is your friend?" Jonathan asks. "The one with the brown hair?"

I nod. "We've been friends since primary school. Things have been a little awkward between us for a while and I was trying to help that a bit." I can't believe I'm saying this.

"Awkward how?" he asks. He's not demanding, just curious, like he actually cares about the answer.

"It's…" I pause and try to arrange my thoughts. "I've had some stuff going on and I feel like we got a bit lost, like we're not on the same page anymore. She can't understand why I gave up riding last year, and then went back to it. And I don't know how to explain it to her."

I've directed Jonathan to Dan's house and I'm grateful when we pull up outside, putting an end to this conversation.

From the street Dan's is a fairly average-looking house. Brick exterior, three-bedroom, two-storey.

We follow a path round the side of the house that's lit by little glowing lights. Well, they'll glow later when it gets dark. At the moment they're reflecting the sunlight more than glowing.

As we round the corner the lawn spreads out before us, a deck leading up to the house to one side, the other direction overlooking the river and farmland.

There's a permanent set-up of fairy lights strung through the trees and eaves of the house, and lanterns are hanging from branches. More lanterns are scattered across tables laden with grazing platters. Near the deck is a table set up with drinks, including an actual punch bowl and bottles of bubbly wine.

We pause at the edge of it all and take a final moment in the shadows before we step into the party.

"Woah," Jonathan breathes. "This is serious business."

I laugh. "I told you … it actually is her business."

We stand there, and I wonder if this is the moment we go back to the conversation we never finished in the car. We managed the whole trip here making small talk. At some point we have to finish that other one … the one about our feelings.

"Hollie!" Dan's mum Natalie calls to me from the deck, and waves for me to follow her as she disappears inside the huge glass sliding door to the kitchen. Apparently we aren't quite as much in the shadows as I thought.

I glance at Jonathan and he's already moving forward, leading me forward into the party.

I head into the house and slide onto a barstool opposite where Natalie is fussing with some kind of fancy food item.

"Hey," I say. "How's it all going?"

"Good, Hollie, it's all good." She smiles. "How are you doing?"

Natalie is one of those people that uses your name all the time in conversation. It makes it impossible not to open up to her. Or maybe it's that she's super nice. Either way, I'm pretty convinced it's her secret weapon in business too.

"I'm doing all right. Had to have the vet out to one of Beth's horses this afternoon, though."

"Oh, honey, that's no good. He doing okay now?"

"Yep, he's all good."

"Oh, sorry!" Natalie turns to Jonathan, who's awkwardly standing in the doorway. "Can I help you with something, love?" She also uses a lot of endearments.

Jonathan shakes his head, looking at me. I assumed he'd be all cool and collected and totally at ease like pretty much all the other times I've seen him, but he definitely isn't right now.

"Oh, my bad," I say. "Natalie, this is Jonathan, Beth's nephew. Jonathan, this is Dan's mum, Natalie."

"Nice to meet you," Jonathan says, his charm suddenly slipping into place like he's pulled on a mask.

"Lovely to meet you too." She turns to me and drops her voice. "My Danny's got no hope if you're spending time with boys like that." She smirks as she continues bustling around the kitchen, opening packets of fancy snack things. Natalie is completely adamant that Dan and I should be dating, despite our repeated affirmations that we are not. Here's hoping she and Kaitlin don't find each other.

I glance in horror at Jonathan, hoping he hasn't heard her, but he's watching out the window and isn't reacting.

"Where is Dan, anyway?" I ask.

Usually Dan is the centre of a party like this, greeting the early arrivals, getting drinks, playing perfect host.

"I don't know," Natalie replies, pulling a tray out of the oven. "Before you go find him, who drove?" I point to Jonathan and Natalie holds out her hand. "I'll need your keys please."

"My keys?" Jonathan hesitates, his hand hovering over his pocket.

I nod. "It's the rules. We're allowed to be here, but keys have to be handed in so Natalie can approve anyone driving home later."

"I know it's a bit batty," Natalie puts in. "But it makes us feel a bit better about a bunch of teenagers crashing our party. You'll get them back later, so long as you haven't been drinking."

Jonathan pulls his keys out and hands them over. "Fair enough."

"Thanks, now go find Danny, and have fun!" She waves us out of the house and we retreat onto the deck.

"His parents don't mind a bunch of teenagers crashing their party?" Jonathan asks as he leans against the deck railing. I select a fancy glass from the drinks table – one that Dan had to rush around after school to collect – and fill it with punch.

"You want some?" I tilt the cup towards Jonathan. "It's non-alcoholic." Jonathan nods and I pass it over before filling another. "And no, they don't mind. It's not an open invite, there's the thing with the keys and Dan's friends are pretty sensible and mature. Dan isn't, but his friends are."

"Oi! I heard that!" I turn as hands land on my shoulders.

"I know you did, that's why I said it." I grin up at Dan.

He ignores me and turns to Jonathan.

"Hey man, how's it going?"

"Not bad," Jonathan replies, casual and confident. "Thanks for the invite."

Dan waves it off, then starts in on the questions: Where did you move from? Why did you move? What's your family like? Is it completely awful having to work with Hollie? The full-scale inquisition.

At his last question I smack Dan on the arm, and Jonathan laughs quietly then says, "No, she's great."

He's looking down at me, the fairy lights reflected in the green of his eyes. My breath catches for a second.

It's going to have to happen.

At some point tonight.

We have to finish that conversation.

But not right now.

I search for something to say to move the conversation elsewhere, and because my mouth is a complete traitor to my heart and brain, the next words that fly out of my mouth leave me feeling sick.

"Is Kaitlin coming?" Cool, another subject I wanted to avoid.

Dan looks at me sideways. I'm more likely to know that than him.

"I'm not actually sure. Connor might have had something on." He shrugs. "What's up with you two this week?"

I fiddle with my cup and sigh, heavily. I avoid looking at Dan and Jonathan.

"She's mad at me … about you. She came over on Monday and accused me of lying to her. I've tried to talk to her … but I can't." The words tumble out and I'm left feeling like I've run several miles. I should have told him earlier. Except I hate how often we have to defend our friendship.

"You should have said," Dan wails. "No wonder you've been feeling shitty this week."

I shrug. "I didn't technically lie to her, and before she even gave me a chance to explain she took off."

"Were you really going to explain?" Dan's eyes flick to Jonathan and I know he's trying not to give away my secrets.

I nod, not trusting my voice not to wobble if I speak. I can feel my eyes growing hot and I blink rapidly, starting to count my breaths.

"She'll come around," he says reassuringly. I nod as though I believe him.

"Um," Jonathan mutters, "isn't that her?"

I spin around and there's Kaitlin, standing at the edge of the lawn, looking edgy and uncomfortable, which isn't like her at all. That's my role in our friendship. She's the confident, outgoing, fun one. Her eyes scan the party guests, who are milling around beside the grazing tables nibbling at cheese and crackers. Eventually her gaze lands on us, then flicks away immediately.

"Maybe now is as good a time as any to talk to her?" Dan says, resting a hand on my shoulder.

I shake my head. "Not at your mum's party."

"But then you'll have it out of the way and you might be

able to enjoy yourself more." He applies the slightest pressure to my shoulder and I step forward involuntarily.

"All right," I sigh. I glance at Jonathan, who's standing beside us looking bewildered. "I need you. Come with me." I grab his sleeve and tug him along behind me, while he exchanges *help me* looks with Dan.

I march across the lawn, wobbling only slightly on my heels, Jonathan trailing in my wake. I reach Kaitlin as Connor approaches from the kitchen, where he must have been depositing his keys with Natalie. I push Jonathan forward.

"Connor, this is Jonathan. He's new here, be nice please." Then I grab Kaitlin's hand and pull her after me. "I need to talk to you." She resists and I slide my hand down, slipping my fingers into hers. I tug gently at our joined hands and her resistance crumbles.

I lead her into the house, heading for the lounge. It's full of people so I head down the hall, shutting the door behind us as we step into a quiet room.

Kaitlin takes it in, staring around at what is clearly Dan's bedroom.

The walls are a soft, warm grey, slightly mottled so it looks like clouds drifting on an overcast day. The bed is covered with a charcoal grey duvet and the curtains are grey too, but the room never feels dull or dreary because scattered all through the room are bright colours. There's a completely random, electric blue cushion shaped like a dolphin on his bed and a red desk lamp, and haphazardly pinned across one wall are several rows of photographs.

Not many people bother with actual physical copies of photos anymore, but Dan does. He prints his favourites and sticks them up on the wall. They're mostly of his family and friends, with the occasional stunning sunset or scenery picture. There's at least fifteen with me in them.

Like most people that enter the room, Kaitlin is drawn directly to the wall.

"Before you jump to any conclusions about me being his girlfriend because I know where his room is: stop." I'm shocked by my audacity. Who even am I? Where did this confidence come from?

She turns to me, face grim, and folds her arms across her chest. She looks ready to take me on in some form of wrestling or martial arts. I'd lose in a second.

I lean back against the door, blocking her only escape unless she fancies jumping out the window, and I'm pretty sure her mini dress combined with the rose bushes outside make it very not worth it. I use the solidness of the wood to ground myself.

"Kait," I say, trying to quell the tremor in my voice. "Please believe me. I am not dating Dan. I promise you."

She glares at me. "Then what's with all your secret 'dates'?" She uses the mocking air quotes at me again and I cringe.

"There's some stuff I do need to tell you, but can I do it tomorrow?" All my energy drains away as the words leave my body, and I'm suddenly exhausted from the confrontation.

I glance up at Kaitlin and she's still staring fiercely at me. I love how fierce she is, except when it's directed at me. I much prefer it when she's using it to protect me, like when we were six and some boy pushed me off the monkey bars because I couldn't get across.

"Please," I whisper. "I want to explain, but I can't do it here. I'll come to yours tomorrow and explain everything. I promise." My eyes are filling more and more with every second she's silent and any moment now the tears are going to spill over.

"Tomorrow," she says finally, and I nod, sniffing a little. "I'm going on that family trip tomorrow at lunchtime, so if you come over about ten, you can tell me what's going on." Her voice is neutral, she hasn't forgiven me yet, but she's going to give me a chance.

I push away from the door. "Thank you," I say.

She smiles, crosses the room and wraps her arms around me. "Whatever it is, Holls, I'm here."

I stiffen in surprise at her contact, then lean into the hug.

Eventually she pulls away, looping her arm through mine and leading me from the room.

"So if you're not dating Danny, does that mean you've got your eye on the new guy?"

I laugh, the sound loud and bright.

Maybe she has forgiven me.

Maybe it's not as hard as I thought it would be.

Maybe my brain is doing that weird thing where it invents bad stories that aren't even true. But, I'll deal with all of those thoughts tomorrow.

For tonight, I'm going to have some fun.

CHAPTER 20

Jonathan

THIS PARTY IS INSANE.

There's a professional band – at a house party.

I haven't heard live music since before Luke's accident … or whatever it was. I've never liked calling it an accident. It's not entirely accurate. It's not like he tripped over a shoelace and ended up with a spinal injury.

After Hollie disappeared into the house with her friend in tow, I was left with Connor, whom I assume is Kaitlin's boyfriend.

We stared at each other, dumbstruck for a moment, before Connor spoke.

"You have any idea?"

"Not a clue," I replied. "I have absolutely no idea about anything."

He laughed, and we fell into conversation. It wasn't as easy as a conversation with Hollie, but it was easier than conversations with any of my friends back home. Connor's a good guy, so far as I can tell. We covered all the small talk subjects, with

Dan dropping in and out as he found time between the jobs his parents kept giving him.

Beth was right. I should be friends with these people. I'm going to have to ditch Jake and Simon and their mates. Hollie's friends are much more stable, and I could do with stable.

Hanging out with Jake and Simon always feels like I'm going to end up in a police station, or at least the principal's office. It's why I try to avoid hanging out with them outside of school. I don't want or need any more attention.

Connor's gone off to find more food for us, since we quickly demolished the fancy platter on the table we claimed in the back corner of the lawn, and I find myself sitting alone, watching the band set up.

The guitarist has this glossy, forest green Gibson, which reminds me painfully of mine, sitting in my old bedroom gathering dust.

My hands twitch and the desire to run my fingers over the strings nearly overwhelms me. I haven't touched a guitar since the accident. Before that night I played every day, usually for hours.

I was given my first guitar when I was six, and it was that instrument that led me to Luke. Even as kids, sent to a school holiday music programme, we had something. He slayed on the drums, I could handle a guitar.

Our friendship was firm and fast.

As the years passed, we learned everything we could about music and playing as many instruments as we could. Then, a couple of years ago, I caught Kristen singing and forced her to start a band with us.

We played open mic nights and school assemblies. We even scored the occasional paying gig, but we were nothing like this band in front of me now. We were a few kids with a drum set, two guitars and a dodgy secondhand keyboard Kris was still figuring out how to play. And now we were nothing, because I destroyed Luke's life.

The band steps onto the little stage built on the grass. It's an impressive scene, with the river cruising slowly past behind them and the sun lowering itself to the horizon. The background music fades out as the band finish tuning their instruments.

The electric guitar twangs and a shiver goes through me. It reminds me of the feeling I get when Hollie touches me. It's wonderful and feels so right, yet is painful at the same time.

The band launches into their first song and I stare at them in disbelief. This is the song Luke and I started our last set with. It's the perfect blend of guitar and drums, and it showcased our talents equally. It's one of the first songs we learned to play together, and I let myself get swept up in it. I rest my chin on my hand and stare out over the river, lost in thoughts from another place, another time.

The bench shifts beside me and I pull myself back to the present to find Hollie sitting beside me.

"Hey," she says quietly.

She's so damn close and it takes everything in me not to rest my head on her shoulder and cry.

I miss my life. My sister, my parents, my school and friends.

I mostly miss my best friend, the one who knew me better than I knew myself. The one who knew exactly how to get me out of a bad mood. The one who was always up for a good time.

"You okay?"

I nod, furrowing my brow. Shouldn't I be asking her that?

She reaches out, and with the lightest brush swipes away a tear I hadn't even realised had fallen.

I let out a long breath. "This song…" I pause, take another breath, stare out over the water so I don't have to look her in those gorgeous blue-grey eyes. I wonder how much I should tell her, how much I can tell her. "This song reminds me of someone. I was having a bit of a moment." I try to smile and brush it off as no big deal.

"It reminds you of Luke?"

I spin to face her, tightness coiling through me.

"What?" My voice is hard, bordering on aggressive. She raises her hands between us.

"Sorry," she whispers. "I thought maybe that's who it reminds you of."

"What do you know about Luke?" I'm growling at her now, like some menacing dog protecting itself.

She rests her hand on my forearm and a shiver races through my body. A very, very good shiver.

"Only that he must have been important to you, because you react strongly every time he gets mentioned. I know something's happened, but I don't know anything else."

"What did Beth tell you?" Rage is simmering. I'm trying to smother it, to remember that shivery feeling, but that's long gone and now there's only a steadily building pressure.

"Beth told me nothing. If you don't want to talk about it, that's okay." I dimly realise she's using the voice she uses to calm the horses when they're worked up and skittish.

Her other hand – the one not resting on my arm – finds mine, which is balled into a fist on the table waiting for the anger to spill over.

She puts her hand over my fist and somehow works her

fingers between mine, releasing the tension there. "If you do want to talk about it though, I'm here, okay?"

I nod. Somehow she's broken through the rage, like I'd been clenching it in my fist. It's dissipating, slowly ebbing away like the tide.

"Yeah." I breathe out the last of the anger. "It was Luke."

Hollie sits silently, waiting to see if I'll continue. "He…" I clear my throat. "He was my best mate. Since we were six. We had this band. He was a master on the drums. It's him playing my ringtone. We used to play this song together and it surprised me." It feels nice to talk about him, but… "And you're right. Something happened, but I can't talk about it, even if I wanted to."

It's true. I can't talk about it. Talking about it would mean telling Hollie everything, and then I'd have to start telling secrets that aren't my own. Even if I never see or speak to Luke again, I'm not going to tell anyone his secrets, not when the last thing he ever said to me was to tell no one.

Hollie squeezes my hand tight. I glance up at her through my stupidly long hair. I need to do something about that. She's opening her mouth, about to say something, when a voice calls out.

"Hey Hollie, Jonathan, come dance!"

I turn towards the voice to see Dan on the edge of the dance floor, absolutely going for it. Kaitlin and Connor are there too, along with a couple of others I've seen at school. Maybe Dan's too caught up in his very energetic dancing to realise we're kind of in the middle of something.

Or maybe he knows exactly what he's doing, like earlier in the parking lot.

"For God's sake, Danny!" Kaitlin reaches out and whacks

him. She gives him a glare and pushes him away from us, further into the crowd now gathered in front of the stage, mouthing "Sorry" in our direction as she does.

Dan turns, looking at us properly.

Hollie's still holding my hand. On top of the table, fingers laced together, for the whole world to see. She's leaning into me. I can feel the shape of her pressed against me, her warm, steady breath keeping me grounded.

Dan has the decency to look sheepish. "Sorry, guys! Ignore me. I didn't say a thing. As you were," he shouts, then turns away and returns to his dancing.

Hollie glances from Dan to me. Her cheeks are flushed and her eyes spark with laughter. "He's such an idiot," she says, total conviction in her voice.

I can only nod in agreement, not sure I'm ready for words. She leans in even closer and I think I might pass out.

"I'm really sorry ... for whatever happened with Luke, for whatever you're going through." Her voice is low and soft and her breath against my cheek sets off the shivers again. I nod and squeeze her hand, but I'm still not sure I'm ready to talk.

We sit in silence for a few minutes, one song blending into the next. The band is killing it and Hollie's friends are enjoying every second.

"You should go dance," I say eventually, gesturing towards the group that is now head banging and air guitaring to a song that really doesn't call for it.

She shakes her head. "I'm okay here with you."

But she's watching them with a tiny smile playing at the corners of her lips.

"Please. Go have fun. I'm sorry, I didn't mean to ruin your night."

She looks over at me, the smile fading away. "You haven't ruined it at all."

Maybe not yet, I think. But if she spends the whole night sitting in the corner with me while I sulk, it'll definitely be ruined by the end.

"Come on then," I say, standing up. There's only one thing for it. Our hands are still clasped and I give them a little tug.

She looks up in surprise. "What? Where?"

I nod to the dance floor. If she's insisting on staying with me then she may as well have a good time. I can mope about Luke any time. And who knows, maybe I'll even have a little bit of fun too.

"Oh, wait," I say, as she gets up from the table and awkwardly steps over the bench in her skirt and heels. "How'd things go with Kaitlin?"

She smiles and I'm filled with relief.

"Good," she says. "We're going to sort everything out tomorrow, but for now we're good. Are you seriously going to come and dance with us?"

I flash her a hurt look. "Was my dancing that bad the other night?"

She blushes – hard – and I desperately want to feel how hot her cheeks are. "No, it's that I can't imagine you'd want to be seen with that lot." She gestures at her friends and I can't help but laugh.

Like every time with Hollie, she's managed to pull me back and lighten my load.

I shrug. "They," I say, "are the least of my concern."

I lead Hollie to the dance floor, and when she hovers shyly at the edge of the group I push her forward with my hand at the small of her back.

Sparks flash, but I douse them. Even though I'm pretty sure I'm in love with her doesn't mean anything is going to happen. It doesn't mean she wants anything to happen. It doesn't mean I'm in any fit state to care about someone properly.

"They're your friends," I murmur, guiding her towards Dan. As much as I really don't want to see them dancing together, it feels like the right thing to do, to get her out of her head. I suspect Dan does for her what she does for me.

Dan spots her, whoops loudly and grabs her hand, pulling her towards him. He locks eyes with me over her head; a silent question. I'm not sure if it's "Is this okay?", "What are you thinking?" or "Why don't you want to dance with her?"

I give him a short nod, then try to lose myself in the music. At least there's plenty of people dancing now and I can blend in easier.

It's different being on this side of the music. My body remembers how to play – and it wants to play – but it doesn't understand why I'm dancing. I can sort of hold my own, but of all the places I could be at this party, up on that stage is the only one that makes any sense.

Except I left music behind with the rest of my life.

I push those thoughts away and catch sight of Hollie. I know it was the right decision to push her out here, to not let her sit in the shadows.

Dan spins her and she tips her head back, laughing. Her blonde hair tumbles down her back, sparkling gold under all the fairy lights. In fact, everything about her right now is sparkling gold.

I want to leave.

I don't want to be here, watching her, knowing I'm already too close and I can't get any closer.

Every time I feel even a sliver of happiness I come crashing back down with the realisation that I don't deserve it.

I ruined someone's life – changed it forever, for the worse.

It wasn't just anyone either. It was *Luke*.

The familiar pain is slicing through my heart, stabbing into my lungs, slashing at my stomach.

My head pounds, the world blurs and I lose track of what's around me.

I hear a scream and sirens and I see the flashing lights.

I clutch at my stomach.

It's happening again.

Somewhere deep down I know it's not real.

Somewhere under all this panic and pain and fear I know that I'm four hours away from where it happened, that it's months later.

A small, warm body presses against me. It hits me with force and lets out a giggle.

I know that sound.

That voice.

My vision clears enough to see Hollie peering up at me, the sparkles in her eyes fading as she takes me in.

She pulls at my hands that are fisted across my abdomen and tangled in the front of my shirt, then reaches up and runs a hand along my jaw.

"Jonathan," she whispers, and somehow I hear her over the music and people around us.

Somehow I hear her over the chaos in my own head.

I shake my head and jerk away from her touch.

All I want to do is stand there and lean into her fingers, feel them caress my face.

But I can't.

I can't drag this beautiful, golden, sparkling girl into the darkness with me. Watching the joy in her eyes die right now simply from looking at me nearly brings me to my knees.

I try to step away.

She holds on tight.

"No," she says. "No. You're not running away. I won't let you."

Her hand slips around my waist and the other goes behind my neck. She pulls my head down to press against her shoulder.

"Don't fight me," she whispers in my ear.

I try to summon the energy to push her away, but there's nothing left, so I let myself do the thing I've wanted to do all week.

I slide my arms around her. I'm hesitant at first, in case she flinches, in case this isn't what she wants.

But she doesn't flinch.

I press my forehead into the curve of her neck and when I inhale I can smell vanilla and maybe a touch of that unique horsey smell I'm always catching whiffs of at Beth's, like crispy hay. She smells exactly like I thought she would, and I hold her tighter.

I return to the moment and realise that she's swaying us gently. The real world starts to creep back into my consciousness.

The beat comes back, and the strum of the guitar, and suddenly I'm back in Dan's backyard, on a dance floor, holding the most beautiful girl I've ever met in my arms.

"You're okay," she says and I nod, head still pressed into her shoulder. I take a shaky breath and lift my head.

"I'm okay," I breathe. "Thank you."

She nods and gives me a small smile. God, her whole body is pressed against mine. Her finger strokes down the back of my neck and without warning molten lava is scorching through my entire body.

My hand finds her cheek without my even thinking it. My thumb brushes along her cheekbone.

Her lips part slightly. She's looking directly into my eyes. Hers are wide, fringed in gorgeous dark lashes and highlighted with shimmering gold make up.

My thumb brushes against her lips and I feel her exhalation against it.

I don't know who moves. I don't know who starts it, but her lips are on mine and mine are on hers. The lava in my bloodstream has turned to fireworks.

The first touch is soft, quick, and we both pause for a mere second, faces millimetres apart. Then our mouths meet again and I may as well melt into a puddle right there, or spontaneously combust.

Either is a real possibility right now.

Kissing Hollie isn't what I thought it would be.

No imagination could make this up.

No one could dream something this good.

One of my hands is holding the sensual curve of her waist and the other is still cupping her cheek. Her hand presses against my lower back, holding me to her. Her other hand slides into the hair at the back of my neck and electricity shoots through me.

My eyes are closed, but everything is going blurry anyway. It's like that feeling I had before, except this is bliss while that was torture.

Torture.

My mind spasms and all I can see inside my head is another kiss.

One that had nothing to do with me.

One that set off the series of events that destroyed everything.

Except that kiss wasn't to blame.

The blame is all on me.

I can't escape it. Not even in these few stolen moments with Hollie.

I pull away, breaking the kiss and stepping back.

The coolness of the night air shocks me.

"No," I say. "We're not doing this."

"What?" She croaks, her voice a husky shell. She's standing before me with stars back in her eyes, but they're dying quickly.

Because that's what I do. I take someone's happiness and destroy it.

I shake my head and step out of reach as she extends her hand towards me.

"We're not doing this." I wave my hands between us. "That was a stupid fucking terrible mistake and it won't happen again."

Then, because I truly am a selfish asshole – like I've warned her – and because I cannot handle seeing whatever pain might be on her face, I spin on my heel and march off the dance floor.

Back to the shadows where I belong.

CHAPTER 21

Hollie

JONATHAN HAS VANISHED.

He's clean disappeared, even though he was in front of me a second ago.

A second before that his body was pressed against mine, one hand on my waist and the other on my face. I can still feel his touch where his thumb brushed along my cheek.

His lips were against mine.

But now he's gone.

If it weren't for the memory of the scorching heat in each place his body touched mine and the tingle in my face where his hand rested, it would be hard to believe what happened a moment ago.

When he led me to the dance floor and pushed me towards Dan, I was so confused.

I thought he was coming to dance with me. I was looking forward to it.

But maybe he was only getting me up to get me away from him.

So I danced with Dan, keeping an eye on Jonathan until I thought he was okay.

He didn't go far. He danced nearby, but not really with us. He stared, his eyes unfocussed, across the crowd as he got lost in the rhythm. I was caught up then too and got lost in the beat. I allowed my worries for Jonathan to slide away with the worries about Kaitlin.

She was right there beside me, putting aside whatever we have to deal with tomorrow. We giggled and spun together, twirling and laughing with our friends.

I lost sight of Jonathan, but then I saw him again, a glimpse across the now-crowded dance floor.

I meant to pull him over to where we were so maybe I'd be able to dance with him, to feel what it would be like for him to put his hands on me like he'd done in Beth's kitchen. Maybe there'd be a bit more.

But when I reached him, stumbling over my own feet in the last steps and crashing into him, his face was twisted in anguish and he was holding his stomach like he'd been stabbed. I looked into his eyes and knew he wasn't really at the party anymore.

Panic attacks. He was having a panic attack and I was hit by the sudden realisation that this wasn't the first one I'd witnessed. My mind flashed to when we were talking in Thea's room.

Instinctively I pulled him into me, intending to hug the panic right out of him.

Apparently, it worked.

Then, a few breaths later, his lips were on mine and that fire that flickered every time he touched me burst into a raging inferno. I was dizzy and breathless by the time he pulled away.

And now he's gone.

I go after him.

He reaches the trees bordering the lawn and I chase him down, grabbing hold of his arm. He spins back to face me.

"That's not good enough," I say, sounding much braver than I feel and way more in control. "Why was it a mistake? What happened? What the hell is going on with you?"

He glares down at me, but I don't think he's really angry. I think he's something else; I just can't figure it out.

"I'm way too fucked up to pull you into my shit," he growls. "I'm not dragging you into this."

I stand my ground – planting my feet, crossing my arms and channeling Kaitlin as much as I can. I glare back at him. "What happened to Luke?"

He jerks like I've slapped him and his face pales.

"Tell me what happened. What's so awful that you think you can act like a jerk and get away with it?"

"Luke's fucking paralysed!" he shouts. "He's got a crushed vertebrae and it was my fucking fault, all right?" His voice increases with each word, the pain in his eyes becoming more evident.

"Your best friend is paralysed, apparently because of you, and you packed up and moved here?" My voice is low and filled with fury.

I'm surprised by it. I don't know where it's come from. But I think of everything I've been through and how I couldn't have done it without my friends, even if most of them had no idea what I was dealing with.

Jonathan nods tightly. "Yeah. Because I'm an asshole." He's not shouting anymore, but his voice is bitter. "We covered that in the beginning, but you wouldn't fucking listen. Go back to your lovely little life with your ponies and your pretend boyfriend and fucking leave me alone."

He turns away again, and this time I'm too stunned by the venom in his voice to follow.

———

I push through the crowded dance floor, shoving people out of my way.

I don't pause.

I don't look around.

I don't want to be stopped.

I don't want to talk to anyone.

I head for the house, straight for the drawer with the car keys. I saw Natalie adding another set when I came inside with Kaitlin so I know exactly where they are.

I haven't drunk any alcohol. I'm fine to drive, but I don't know what Dan's done with my keys. They're not in the drawer with everyone else's.

I pull Jonathan's set from the tangle. I know they're his because of the guitar keyring and the old-fashioned key I know opens Beth's back door.

I run my finger over the keyring. A guitar makes sense after his revelation earlier.

There's so much more to him I don't know. My knowledge barely skims the surface.

And stupidly, I want to know.

Even after he screamed at me, I want to know everything there is to know about him.

Is he really the snarky jerk he's acting like, or is there someone else hiding behind all that?

Mostly I want to know what hurts him so badly. I'm desperate to know what happened to him even though he clearly doesn't want to share, even with me.

I clench my fist around the stupid guitar keyring, feeling it dig into my palm, and march out the sliding door. I skirt around the edge of the deck and slide into the shadows.

I'm filled with rage, hurt and embarrassment, and they're taking turns sitting at the top of my consciousness.

My hands shake and it takes a couple of tries to line the key up with the lock on his stupid old-fashioned car.

I finally manage it and wrench the door open, dropping into the seat. I slam the door and the raging part of me feels a little better.

The car rumbles to life and I jerk at the seatbelt, fighting with the locking mechanism.

Then gravel is crunching satisfyingly under the tyres and I pull out onto the road.

It's deserted, as I expected. It's not exactly a city street. The final sounds of the band fade as the anger subsides.

I feel heat on my cheek and realise it's a loose tear. I swipe at it, then grasp the steering wheel tightly. It's the only thing that's anchoring me.

This stupid piece of leather in this stupid car owned by a stupid boy.

Except he's not stupid and you know it, the little voice in my head whispers. The voice is right. He's not some stupid boy, and deep down I know he's not really a jerk either. I can't let that belief go.

I think about all the things he's done for Beth and wonder if maybe moving here was as much about her as it was about escaping his past. I remember the look on his face when I found him sitting at that picnic table, staring out over the river.

That wasn't the face of some sneery jerk. That was the face of someone in pain. I know. I've seen it enough in my own mirror.

There are more tears on my face now, but I don't wipe them away. What's the point?

I let them fall.

Maybe I should go back. Even if he doesn't want to be kissing me, maybe he still needs me. He needs a friend, and he doesn't seem to have any of them here besides me.

My foot eases off the gas pedal and the car's speed drops slightly. There's an intersection ahead where I can turn around.

I'll go back.

I'll put aside whatever feelings I have about that kiss. I'll be his friend, whether he wants that or not.

I wouldn't let him run away from me before. I'm not going to run away from him. Not when he needs someone.

I'm slowing down as I approach the intersection.

There's another set of headlights.

They flare in my vision.

A metallic screech.

A crunch.

Everything is spinning.

I scream.

CHAPTER 22

Jonathan

I TAKE a swig from the bottle in my hand, but it's already empty.

I sigh and toss it aside. It clinks accusingly against the other bottles lying in the sun-bleached grass beside me. I'm being judged by empty bottles, and I tell their judgement where it can go.

I reach for another, but my stash is gone. I'll have to go and find more, but the thought of navigating my way through all those people is enough to make me stay where I am.

"Dude." There's a sliding noise and a body lands heavily on the bank next to me. "Oomph. Okay, you're here, where's Hollie?" Dan looks around as if Hollie's going to appear out of one of the bushes.

After I freaked the fuck out and left her stricken on the dance floor, I swiped a handful of beer bottles and went back to hide in the shadows.

Shame and regret swirled around me in a dark cloud. I never wanted to hurt her, especially not like that.

Lurking under a huge tree in the far back corner of the

lawn, I peered down the bank, wondering if it was possible to get to the river's edge from Dan's back lawn.

There was a faint trail through the grass and bushes clinging to the edge so I followed it, down to a small clearing.

It seemed as good a place as any to lick my wounds and stew over what I'd done – and down several bottles of beer in quick succession.

The party carried on behind me, the music floating out over the river on the light summer breeze.

The beer was a poor choice, which I knew when I took it and with every mouthful I swallowed. It's never made anything better.

I fall back onto the grassy bank and close my eyes as the stars spin and swirl above me.

I think about what would have happened if I hadn't pushed Hollie away. If instead I'd brought her here to lie under the stars. I could have told her all my secrets in the dark.

Except I can't tell her my secrets without telling her Luke's.

And I'm back to square one.

Stuck living with this thing that I can't share, not without betraying him.

Even if I had told her despite my promise, I can imagine how she would have reacted; the way her brows would have scrunched together as she looked at me with disappointment.

It was bad enough when she had a go at me for bailing on my best friend when most people would think he needed me most. But what people don't understand is that Luke couldn't even look at me anymore.

The reason I left was because Luke wanted me to go.

"I don't know where Hollie is," I mutter. I shove a hand into my hair and think of her again, and her laugh as she mocked me for my stupid habit. I yank on the dark strands instead.

"Man, have you been drinking?" Dan's spotted the bottles.

"So?"

"Aren't you driving?" He reaches over and gives me a shove, but it's not an aggressive one. It's the kind of shove guys who are friends give each other when they care.

"I'll sleep in my car," I say with a shrug. Why does he even care?

"Aren't you driving Hollie?"

"Highly unlikely," I scowl, and push myself to sitting. I feel too vulnerable to have this conversation lying down. "Isn't her car here, anyway? Isn't she driving that home?" The steely edge in my voice shouldn't surprise me, but it does. After all this time I should have got used to biting back with anger when other people are simply trying to be normal. They never seem to realise they're dealing with someone who isn't normal.

Dan flings a filthy glare in my direction. It's completely deserved, but I still bristle.

"I was planning to use it tomorrow." He's angry.

I don't say anything, and we take in the night for a few minutes. "What happened?" he asks eventually.

I glance in his direction to find him watching me carefully.

"Nothing," I growl. "I'm sure Hollie will manage fine. Can't she stay here? With you?" That would be the best option, I realise. Hollie stays here with Dan and realises that he, who is clearly a good guy and not at all fucked up, is who she wants to be kissing.

"I know she really likes you," he says. His low, steady voice is a stark contrast to the aggression in my own. "In whatever capacity, she does really care, and I'm looking out for her, okay?"

"She shouldn't," I snap, yanking on my hair again. "Look," I begin. I'm about to tell him to piss off and leave me alone, to go and convince Hollie she's better off not caring about me, when I'm interrupted by a phone ringing.

Dan pulls his phone out of his pocket and glances at the screen, then at me, a look of confusion on his face.

"Hollie?" he says as he answers the call. I sit straighter, both desperate to know – and dreading hearing – what she's about to tell him.

"Woah, woah. Slow down. What happened?"

Hollie speaks for a while. I can hear her muffled voice coming from the phone speaker, but I can't make out the words.

"It's okay, Holls," Dan says, voice calm and soothing. The tension in me ratchets up again. Something's happened. "I'll be right there."

She says something else, her volume rising, but I still can't make out what she's saying. Then I'm sure I hear the crack in her voice as she breaks down sobbing. I push my hands into my eyes.

I did this.

I did this to her.

"No, he's right here," Dan is saying, and I peer up at him from between my fingers. He's watching me as he listens to Hollie crying. "No, Hollie. It's okay. It'll all be okay. I'll tell him. We're coming now, okay? I'll see you real soon."

His voice is so calm, so soothing. Except with every word he says I feel myself winding tighter.

I want to scream, hit something, unleash it.

I most definitely want to run away before he ends that call and lets rip at me for what I've done to her.

As I move to get up his voice stops me. The soothing, gentle voice he used with Hollie is gone. This voice is expressionless – devoid of any emotion, good or bad.

"She's been in an accident."

I slump back onto the bank.

Everything goes numb.

Dan's still talking and I try to focus on his words. I can barely process anything except the word "accident" spiralling in my head.

"She's mostly okay, I think. She said something about her leg. She said she's sorry."

"She's sorry?" I turn to him, incredulous. "What is she sorry for?"

She's not to blame for this.

I've done it again.

I hurt her and treated her like crap, so she left the party.

And had an accident.

God, I should have stayed away from her in the first place.

I should have picked up the horse shit and fixed the stupid fence and stayed the hell away from her. Then none of this would have happened.

The numbness is wearing off, and as it goes it's peeling off the thinly healed scab over the wounds inflicted last December.

Dan gets up and begins climbing the bank.

"You need to come with me," he says. I'm about to argue but he cuts me off. "Because she was driving your car."

CHAPTER 23

Jonathan

THERE'S a knock on my door and I manage to lift my head far enough off my mattress to see Beth peering around the edge of the door frame.

The exertion of holding my head up is too much and I let it drop again, letting out a small groan as the pounding intensifies.

"You're still alive in here, then?"

"Unfortunately," I grumble, burrowing under the duvet.

I feel rotten. Every part of me.

My mouth is dry and dusty, my head throbs and there's this debilitating weight pinning me to the bed.

"Big night, huh?" Beth says, stepping into the room. She's trying to be funny, I think. Trying to keep the mood light. But she's always been so careful about encroaching on my personal space, so coming into my room right now feels like a big deal.

I groan in response.

There's something digging me in the back and I wriggle around until my hand wraps around my phone.

I don't remember falling asleep.

I remember lying here in the dark, clutching my phone and wishing for something, but the details are all foggy.

"I don't suppose you've heard from Hollie?" It's a simple question, but my breath catches at the sound of her name.

I have a sudden, *very* vivid recollection of kissing her under a million fairy lights.

My mind jumps from that image of her, sparkling golden, to the image of my car parked sideways in a ditch, the front corner crumpled.

"It's only that it's after one, and she usually comes on a Saturday morning. I haven't heard from her at all," Beth is saying. "I'm a bit worried about her. She's got some stuff going on and this is so unlike her."

It's after one? Shit. I've slept the day away.

Which is probably for the best, because at least when I'm asleep I don't have to remember.

"Shit," I say, forcing myself upright. My head pounds again and I press my fingers into my eyes, willing it to stop. "She was in an accident." My voice is rough, crackling over the words, breaking on the last one. I take a gasping breath. "I was meant to tell you. I'm sorry. They took her to hospital. My car's probably a write-off." Not that my car matters at all.

Beth freezes a few steps from my bed, her face turning white.

"Accident?" She's taking in my dishevelled state and my obvious hangover. I groan into my hands.

The night is coming back to me in flashes and I'm putting the snippets together.

Her holding my hand as I told her all I could about Luke.

The kissing.

Oh my God, the *kissing*. The utter bliss, the fierce burning, the dizziness.

Pushing her away.

Shouting.

Drinking.

The phone call to Dan.

"I'm so sorry, Beth," I croak, and there are trails of heat and wet on my face.

"You drove after you'd been drinking?" Beth's voice is tight and she's glowering down at me now. "And you drove drunk with Hollie in your car? I know you've got stuff going on, Jonathan, but this isn't okay! I thought you knew better!" Beth isn't a yeller by nature. I'm not sure I've ever heard her yell, but she is now, and I'm not even sure why. I flinch when she uses my real name, not the nickname she's called me my whole life.

"No! I didn't drive. Of course I didn't drive drunk!" I'm verging on yelling too, then with a concerted effort I lower my voice. "I'm an idiot and an asshole and many other awful things, but no, I wouldn't do that. Ever."

"But you said your car is a write-off?"

"It probably is. Not that it matters. I don't care about the car. But I wasn't driving; Hollie was."

She deflates. Her anger vanishes.

"Hollie was driving," she says quietly. I nod. "Are you hurt?"

I shake my head. "I wasn't in the car." My voice breaks again and my hands burrow into my hair.

Beth perches on the edge of my bed. "Johnny, what happened?"

"She was upset," I start. I can't look at her. Shame hits me like a tidal wave. It was my fault she was upset. "She took my car and left. I didn't even know she'd gone until she rang Dan after the accident. We got there as they were getting her out of the car." The screech of metal as they pried the door off the car and extracted her was still ringing in my ears. "Another car hit her. I think they were drunk. I don't know. They took Hollie in an ambulance and Dan's mum went with her. Her leg. There was something wrong with her leg." I'm rambling and random half sentences are falling out of my mouth. "I don't know anything else."

As I stop talking and exhale whatever air is left in my lungs, my body starts to shake. I wrap my arms around my waist, clutching at the pain that's settled there. I'm convulsing, gasping for breath.

Beth's arms come around me and I lean into her, giving into the sobs tearing at my throat.

"I'll ring her mum and find out what's happening," she says quietly into my ear, smoothing back my hair. It's a very motherly thing to do, and not something anyone, even my own mother, has done in years. It's not like I gave her many opportunities. "Do you have your insurance details, or any details of what happened to the car last night?"

I shake my head about the insurance, but reach for a slip of paper on the bedside table. Details of the tow truck company are scribbled across it.

She pulls me back into her when I hand her the paper, but I resist. I'm seventeen and crying on my aunt's shoulder. It's horrifying.

She holds on tight though, and I give up fighting. As mortifying as it is, it feels good to have an adult take control. I cry myself out, and she finally releases her hold. "I'll ring your mum," she says.

"But I'm fine," I blurt, shock hitting me.

She's going to send me home.

Oh, God, she's going to send me back.

My breath is stuck again, but thankfully the tears are already drained.

I try to say more, try to apologise, try to beg her to let me stay and promise I'll never cause her a moment of stress or worry ever again.

Beth pauses at the doorway and turns back to me.

"Go have a shower or something; you'll feel better," she says, not unkindly. "Then we'll deal with this car."

She walks out of the room, leaving me in the semi-darkness.

There's light trying to creep in around the curtains and it leaves the room a hazy grey.

I look around. I haven't even had a chance to put a poster on the wall, but the thought of leaving this new home is terrifying.

I'll have to go back. There's nowhere else to go.

Back to the bedroom filled with dusty guitars and memories of Luke.

Back to school with all my old friends because I failed at getting away. I couldn't even scrape together a life for myself here.

My phone buzzes on the bed next to me and I snatch at it even though I don't know who could be texting me. Surely it won't be one of the very few people I want to hear from right now.

It's a message from an unknown number.

> Hey man. Hope you're doing okay and that the car isn't too bad. Hollie's got a broken leg and some bruising, but otherwise fine. She's going home this afternoon. Dan.

I don't know how he got my number, but I breathe a sigh of relief.

A broken leg. It could be worse.

Hot shame rushes over me.

Yeah, it could be worse, but if I hadn't been an asshole to her she'd be completely fine right now.

My room is suddenly suffocating. I crawl out of bed and wrench the curtains open. The sun is blinding, overexposing the room.

My backpack is dropped on the floor beside the small table I've been using as a desk, waiting for me to deal with the homework that's due Monday.

I give it a kick. As if homework or anything to do with school matters.

Kicking it feels so good I pick it up and throw it. It slams into the floor.

I bang the door as I leave the room, slamming my fist into it, then crash into the bathroom, wrenching the shower control to full blast and absolutely scalding.

The last thing I hear as I step under the stream of water is Thea's cry.

I wince. I forgot about the baby. I've upset her now too.

I stand under the burning water and let it mix with a new stream of tears.

CHAPTER 24

Hollie

MY LEG IS THROBBING.

It feels too big for the cast they've put around it, and with every beat of my heart it pulses, dragging pain through my leg.

I try to move, to readjust the angle of the leg, but my shoulder screams at me with the movement. I've got one heck of a bruise from the seatbelt and the doctors said the bruising I can't actually see will be as bad, if not worse.

But they all said I was lucky.

Lucky I wasn't a second or two faster, which would have had the other car hitting me squarely in the driver's side door. Apparently a broken leg and some bruises is pretty good for being hit by a drunk driver.

I don't feel lucky.

Aside from the physical pain, I don't feel much at all.

I'd have thought I'd feel something, but everything has felt numb since they lifted me into the ambulance last night.

That was the moment I saw Dan and Jonathan, staring in horror at the car skewed sideways into the ditch, the door lying on the ground next to it, the pristine vehicle now a crumpled wreck. I tried to call out to Jonathan, to apologise, to somehow make amends.

A cop had already questioned me briefly about what happened, and who the car belonged to and why was I driving it.

It was in that moment I realised I'd not only crashed Jonathan's car, I'd stolen it too.

The cop didn't seem too concerned about my grand theft auto, but then I hadn't exactly told him I'd stolen it. I told him it belonged to my friend … which I guess was a lie too.

But I tried calling out to Jonathan, though my shout was cut short by the searing pain across my chest from the bruise that was already forming.

Natalie, who'd appeared with the boys, hushed me, watching as the paramedics prepared to lift me.

Jonathan turned towards me and flinched. His face shut down, the look of horror covered by a mask of empty cold.

I shove the memory of that expression out of my head.

A glass of water appears beside my face and Dan hands over my selection of painkillers and anti-inflammatories. He sits cautiously on the couch, careful not to jostle me.

He's so bloody considerate it makes me want to throw things, except that I can't be bothered picking anything up, let alone throwing it.

Why can't I have dreams about kissing him instead of Jonathan, who seems determined to win the title of Biggest Jackass Ever before he turns eighteen? It's a pointless road for my thoughts to travel. The way I think of Dan and the way I think of Jonathan are so far apart. Those lines will never blur.

I swallow the pills with a gulp of water.

"Thanks," I croak, leaning back into the cushions.

I was home from the hospital for less than an hour before Dan was at my door.

He took one look at me and wrapped me in an extremely gentle hug.

Though I'd seen him at the accident scene, we hadn't spoken. He stayed with Jonathan on the far side of the road as the police spoke to Jonathan, I assume about his car.

I try not to think of it as a betrayal. I know Jonathan needed someone, but it still hurt a teeny bit.

Dan nestles in next to me and props his feet on the coffee table. I can't help but lean into him. He's steady, he's constant and he already knows all my secrets.

"What happened, Holls?" He says it quietly, barely a whisper, giving me the opportunity to pretend I didn't hear him.

With great pain, I slowly turn my head and rest it on his shoulder. His hand reaches over and takes mine.

"I kissed him," I whisper back. I squeeze my eyes closed. "Or he kissed me. I don't know. There was kissing."

I can't say more. A gaping chasm has opened in my chest. I'm desperate to cry, but I'm too scared of the physical pain I'll endure when my body is overrun with sobs. My lip quivers.

"I feel like that should be a good thing," he whispers into my hair, "not something that should make you cry."

I tilt my head in a tiny nod, and the pain flares again.

"I'd have thought so too." I sigh. "But then he stopped it, told me it could never happen, yelled at me and disappeared."

"Disappeared to go get trashed," Dan growls, then squeezes my hand. We're silent for a breath and when he speaks again the frustration is gone from his voice. "I feel like there's something going on with him."

"Yeah," I breathe. "I don't know exactly what, though."

Another silence.

I'm processing what to say next when Dan asks me what it was like.

"What was what like? Being in a car crash? Wouldn't recommend." I'm trying to be funny. I'm failing, but he laughs anyway.

"No, I meant, kissing him. What was that like?"

"Oh." I was trying not to think too much about it since I'd so clearly and painfully been rejected. I squish my eyes shut and feel a tear squeeze out onto my cheek. "Amazing," I say simply.

I feel his head move as he nods.

"Why'd you leave?" he asks.

I don't know the answer to this.

I don't know why I didn't find Dan, or Kaitlin, and cry on their shoulders.

I don't know why I didn't pretend it hadn't happened and carried on dancing.

I don't know why I didn't push Jonathan for more or why I let him run out on me.

"I wanted to go home. I wanted to be alone. I didn't want everyone to see me cry."

"I don't mind seeing you cry, Holls," he says with a squeeze of my hand. "Obviously I don't *like* seeing you cry, because I wish you didn't have too, but if you need to, I'm always here."

"I know you are, and I appreciate it, and everything you've done for me. But I'm such a burden on everyone." More tears find their way to my cheeks, making trails down my skin. "I didn't want to ruin your night, which I suppose I did anyway."

"Hollie." Dan pulls away slightly so he can turn to look down at me. He lifts my chin with his fingertips. "You'll never be a burden. You don't have to do this alone."

I nod.

But I don't really believe him.

CHAPTER 25

Hollie

THE DAYS ALL BLUR TOGETHER.

I think it's Friday again. A week since the accident.

The pain in my leg is a dull, ever-present ache. It's the same with the bruising across my shoulder. My neck is stiff from whiplash and I have a constant headache.

The weather seems to have shifted with my life, from balmy late summer days to days of gloomy drizzle. I can't remember what day it started, but the world is now tainted with the grey haze of persistent rain and the humidity is sticky and damp.

I'm sprawled on the couch flicking through Netflix, unable to make a decision on what to watch.

I haven't been to school. I can barely make it to the bathroom from my nest on the couch, let alone get around school – especially with the rain.

Crutches and slippery wet floors aren't a good combination. Or that's what I tell Mum each day when she tries to get me to go.

So I've spent the week nestled on the couch, bingeing so

many TV shows and movies I can't actually remember what I've watched.

Dan's been here every day after school. He brings me homework and gossip.

I ignore both the homework and the gossip.

He's trying and I love him for it, but at the moment not even his eternal optimism can bring me back.

"Did you see him?" I interrupted some story Dan was telling me about what happened at lunch on Tuesday or Wednesday. I can't remember which day, and I don't care that I was rude.

I wasn't even listening to the story because I was thinking about Jonathan.

I'm furious with him for breaking my heart, and at the same time I fully understand why he did what he did.

He said it was because of him, but I'm pretty sure he understands I'm not worth the effort.

Dan watched me carefully for a moment, then nodded.

"He's been at school but I haven't spoken to him." He looked wary, as if he wasn't sure he should be telling me this. "He looks pretty rough."

I nodded, unsure what to make of that, unsure what to say next. So I let it go, and so did Dan.

Scrolling the TV menu has lost its appeal, so I drop the remote onto my stomach and stare at the ceiling for a while.

I'm such a waste of space.

Useless…

Lazy…

Miserable…

A burden…

The thoughts line up and file through my head, a steady stream of bitterness trudging through my mind.

If I was better, funnier, happier, something *more*, then Jonathan would have wanted to keep kissing me.

Kaitlin wouldn't have spent the whole of last week furious with me, and this week too, I suppose, since I missed our date on Saturday morning to explain everything, and by the time they'd found my phone in the car and got it back to me she'd stopped messaging to ask where I was. She hasn't responded to any of my apologetic messages.

I even managed to completely fail Beth. Beth, who gave me a job doing something I loved.

I won't be able to ride or work for weeks, and even when I'm better she won't want me back. She only took me on in the first place because she felt sorry for me and Mum had talked her into it.

I wasn't even that good at riding. Beth was simply too nice to say so.

There's a little voice trying to claw its way to the surface, but it's somewhere far in the recesses of my mind, drowning under the negativity.

The voice clings on tight, telling me that none of that is true.

It's reminding me that I'm not broken, that I'm not useless.

You're sick, it says.

Remember what Dana taught you, it says.

Dana. My counsellor. The one I've been seeing every week since Dan came to my house and got me out of bed after my first depressive episode.

The voice fights against the tide of negative comments, reminding me how to deal with this, and that I can get better.

But I'm tired, and so is that lone little voice that tells me I'm worth it.

A lonely voice against a crowd of millions.

It slips, loses its grip and falls back into the landslide of despair.

Falling.

Falling.

Falling.

———

I wake to the sound of voices.

I am – unsurprisingly – on the couch. My pink fleece blanket is sliding off me, pooling on the floor. It leaves a cool chill on the parts of me left exposed.

Mum can't understand why I want the huge blanket in the summer heat, but it's much more for emotional comfort than temperature control.

I blink a few times and the ceiling pendant comes slightly more into focus.

Everything seems a bit blurry around the edges these days.

I wonder if I'm supposed to tell someone about that. But I had no signs of head injury from the accident and the doctors didn't tell me to keep an eye out for them. It feels like something I've experienced before, but I can't put my finger on it.

The voices are muted, coming from the kitchen. I can't tell whose they are, or what they're talking about. No doubt it's about me though, because that's all anyone does around here. Murmur about me while giving me sideways glances when they come to the house to visit.

It's got to be Mum, because who else would be in the house? But I can't place who she's with.

I glance at the clock. 3:36 pm. It'll be Dan then, bringing me my daily dose of homework and updates. Not that I'm interested in either.

I only want to know about Jonathan; if he's given any indication that he doesn't completely hate me for writing off his car.

But Dan doesn't talk about him and I don't know how to ask again.

I'm not even sure if I can handle hearing the truth. I know Dan won't lie to me, so he must be avoiding the subject because it might make me feel worse.

As I lie here thinking about him, Dan's face appears around the edge of the door. He flashes me a smile, though I'm not sure what there is to smile about.

I'm a frightful mess, there's no way around that.

Showering with my leg is a total pain, so I haven't been doing much of it.

I give Dan a little wave, then drop my hand listlessly back onto my stomach.

God, everything is so exhausting.

Dan's face disappears for a moment, then he enters the room, closely followed by my mother.

This isn't going to go well, I think, noting the determined expressions on their faces. Dan's jaw is tight and the way he's looking at me with those deep brown eyes of his, I know he's going to ask me to do something.

And the thing is, those eyes … they're nearly impossible to say no to.

"Hey," I say, determined not to walk into any trap they're about to set for me.

Dan sits on the coffee table. Mum perches on the end of the couch, by my feet. She looks nervous and worried, and I feel a flash of guilt for inflicting even more pain and stress on her.

She hasn't had it easy, but she's been a great mum, even if she is a bit of a workaholic, and I try to stay out of trouble.

That is until I stole a car and crashed it.

Dan reaches over and takes one of my hands in his.

"Hollie, it's time you started doing something again," he says. His voice is low and calm, like the one I use with the horses when they're spooked. He's holding some serious eye contact and I pull away, looking instead at my toes peeking out the end of my cast.

"Not much I can do at the moment," I say. I'm trying to be flippant, but it falls flat.

He squeezes my hand and some unseen force makes me look at him again.

"You can be doing more than you are. You *need* to be doing more than you are."

He looks down at our hands and bites his lip. He squeezes my hand again and inhales to speak, but nothing comes out. Instead he shakes his head and throws my mum a helpless glance.

Woah, he *is* worried.

"Honey," Mum says, resting a hand on my leg. I can hear the strain in her voice. "You need to be keeping up with the things that help your depression." There's a little crack in her voice but she manages to hold it together. "We're worried about you."

Dan nods his agreement.

"You need to start getting up and out again, because you're slipping back, Hollie." His eyes are brimming with tears.

Oh God. I've never seen him cry. Not Daniel.

"It's really hard, though," I whisper, tears filling my own eyes. I don't want to hurt him, or Mum. I don't want to scare them either. "I thought it was to do with the accident."

"We know it's hard, honey," Mum says. "But you're not doing it alone. We're here to help you."

"Everything's fallen apart," I whisper, my voice breaking as I think about Kaitlin, and Beth, and Jonathan.

I turn away.

I can't look at them, staring at me with sadness in their eyes and worry etched on their faces.

"I'm sorry," I sob, and the tears spill over.

Dan's here in a second, on his knees beside the couch, wrapping me in his arms and pressing my head against his shoulder.

It's such a beautiful feeling, even with the aches and pains from the bruises splashed across my torso.

I realise I haven't been hugged, or held in any way, since the day after the accident. Every time Dan's tried to, I've avoided the contact. I didn't realise how much I missed it or how much I needed it, and I cry even harder.

"We got you, gorgeous," Dan murmurs into my hair. "You've got this. You can do this. You have got nothing to be sorry for."

I lean into my friend. His warm, solid arms are around me as his hand strokes down my spine in a soothing rhythm, and I let the tears fall.

"I am, though," I say as the tears finally dry up. "I'm sorry that I didn't realise, I'm sorry that I made you both worry. I thought it was the accident."

"We thought the same too, for a little bit," Mum says. "But we realise now that it's not, and so today, you're going out."

I push away from Dan and stare at my mother in horror.

"Out?" I ask, incredulous. "Out where?"

"Well, you can either go somewhere with me, or with Dan. I don't really care which or where you go, but you need to go out."

"I'm not up for that," I mutter, and the incredulity has already vanished, because emotions are *exhausting*.

"You are," Dan says, clearly not taking no for an answer. "And I have an excellent idea if you come with me."

I sigh, heavily. "Is there any way at all you'll let me out of this?"

They both laugh softly, shaking their heads, and I'm quite mad that my best friend is such a freaking delightful human that he can charm anyone into doing anything. Even me.

I sigh dramatically and push myself off the couch.

"First things first," Mum says, still smiling. "You need a shower."

CHAPTER 26

Hollie

"NO. NO. NO," I say, clutching at the car door. "No!"

Dan glances over at me bracing myself in the passenger seat of his car, fighting the urge to rip open the door and make a run for it.

"You don't want to see Milo, Harley and Alaska?" His expression is confused. He's brought me here to see the horses, not the people who live here. But Beth and Jonathan are probably at home and I'm not sure I can handle seeing them, even from a distance.

I do miss the horses, though.

Dan stops the car in the driveway, giving me a moment. I'm pretty sure there's no alternative to this field trip I've been forced to go on, or if there is, it'll for sure be worse than this option.

I think of Milo, of little Harley with his huge attitude, and my gentle giant Alaska, who of course isn't mine at all.

"What about Beth?"

"What about her?"

"She's mad at me. I bailed on her. I let her down when she really needed my help."

"Hollie." Dan reaches over and holds my hand. "She's not mad. She's not upset with you, not even a little bit. She's worried about you. She thought you'd have been to visit by now."

"You don't know that."

"But I do, because she rang your mum this morning to see how you were doing." He takes a breath, bracing himself for whatever he's going to say next. "Whatever your head is telling you, it's wrong."

Oh.

I think over what he's said.

He wouldn't lie to me. He wouldn't bring me here if Beth was mad.

I can't trust my own brain right now, but I can always trust Dan.

"You want to do this?" he asks, squeezing my hand.

I squeeze back and nod.

Yes. I'm going to do this. Not necessarily for me, but for Dan and for Mum.

And seeing the horses can't be all bad. In fact, I'd say that's going to be a pretty big highlight. I've missed them, and maybe they've missed me too.

The tiniest crack has appeared in the gloomy haze that's clouded my mind for the past week.

It's only a microscopic sliver, but maybe ... maybe I can get through this again.

Dan eases the car down the driveway and I force myself to focus on the familiar surroundings, not the anxiety of seeing Jonathan if he happens to be here.

Two ducks are paddling on the pond in the front paddock.

The trees lining the driveway are fading from their lush summer green into the fiery colours of autumn.

The gravel crunches beneath the tyres and it's strangely comforting.

The house comes into view, then the barn, yards and arena. The three horses are grazing in the paddock right between the barn and arena, their covers tossed over the railing fence. Their coats gleam in the sun, which has made a sudden reappearance this afternoon.

Jonathan's car is parked by the barn. The dark green paint is pristine, except that driver's side front corner where the steel is mangled and twisted. The driver's door leans against the car, completely detached, because they had to wrench it clean off the car to get me out.

The screech of metal tearing flashes through my mind.

My gut twists.

Maybe I was lucky, like the doctors said.

I can't look anymore, and tear my gaze away from the wreckage. Maybe I do need to see Jonathan today, so I can apologise.

Not that I feel ready for that.

I glance around, looking for something else to focus on.

My car is sitting in the place I usually park it, under the big tree by the barn.

"Why's my car here?" I turn to Dan, confused.

"Your mum lent it to Beth, for Jonathan. Until they figure out if his is repairable."

"Oh," I say. "I guess that makes sense."

The anxiety about seeing Jonathan is growing.

My heart is racing, my breathing is growing shallow and my hands start to shake.

I look back to the horses.

Harley has raised his head in our direction, watching the car approach.

I really have missed them. I think of the way they smell, which is both gross and amazing at the same time. I think of the softness of their muzzles and the way their manes tangle around my fingers.

The anxiety fades a little.

Dan parks the car and I reach into the backseat for my crutches. They've fallen to the floor and I can't quite get to them.

I sigh with frustration and flop back into the seat, hot tears stupidly prickling at my eyes.

"This is too damn hard," I mutter.

"I know it's hard," Dan says, pulling my door open in time to hear my complaining. He hands me the crutches and helps me out of the car. It's a long way up when you've only got the use of one leg.

I make my way awkwardly to the fence. The three horses spot me and amble in my direction, nickering softly.

Harley reaches me first, ploughing his head into my chest and bunting me gently.

"Hey, boy," I croon, stroking his cheek. He huffs warm horsey breath into my hands. "You missed me, huh? I missed you too, you little rascal. I hope you've been behaving for Beth."

There's the sound of more tyres on gravel and my heart leaps into my throat, anxious that it's Jonathan.

Then I realise he's already here somewhere, because my car is here.

I turn and see a gleaming black SUV towing an empty trailer crawling up the driveway. It pulls up next to Dan's car and parks.

A woman gets out of the driver's seat and a teenage girl climbs down from the backseat.

There's someone in the front passenger seat but they make no move to get out. The woman heads directly for the house.

"Hi," the girl calls out, waving at us. She's vaguely familiar, but I can't place her.

She's wearing a bright red t-shirt and tight black jeans. Her dark hair is piled up on her head in a messy topknot. She's gorgeous and carries herself with easy confidence. The girl strolls towards us, pushing her sunglasses up onto her head.

"You're not Beth or Johnny," she says with a grin. She's studying me, then she turns her attention to Dan. Her face lights up as she turns back to me.

"Are you Hollie?" She's nearly squealing, and I realise exactly who this is.

"Kris!" The voice breaks through the sticky afternoon heat. It's a male voice, strained and possibly in pain. Dan automatically goes for the car.

"Kris," the voice calls again. "I need to get out ... *now!*"

"Shit, sorry!" Kris calls back and hurries for the car. She reaches it at the same time as Dan, who must have his Good Samaritan hat on today.

Kris pulls a set of crutches from the backseat and hands them to the person in the front, then helps him to slowly ease out of the vehicle.

It looks much easier getting down from the high SUV than it was getting out of Dan's sedan.

I'm moving towards them as fast as I can, but I'm still too far away to hear what they're saying to each other. She's steadying him, a hand on his arm as he adjusts his weight on the crutches. He has no cast on his leg like I do, so his injury isn't immediately noticeable.

Kris gives him a thumbs up. When he nods, she steps away and comes back to me.

Dan's staring at the other guy, and I don't really blame him.

He's gorgeous.

As in, should be in European perfume ads.

His face is all angles, with sharp cheekbones and a striking jaw. He's got dark eyes and dark hair that's cropped short around the sides, a bit longer on top. The sky-blue t-shirt he's wearing sets off the warm brown of his skin.

I've seen him somewhere before.

He gazes around the yard, taking in the house, the horses, the barn and finally Jonathan's car. He winces visibly when he sees that.

He moves to take a step, and stumbles.

I gasp.

Kris is facing me. I see her eyes widen and a look of terror cross her face as she whirls back – in time to see Dan step forward and catch him.

"Woah," Dan says, slipping an arm around the other guy's back, steadying him. "You okay?"

The two boys stare at each other for a moment too long before the newcomer glances away.

"Yeah. Thanks. I got it," he grits out.

Dan nods and eases his arm back. This time when the dark-haired boy takes a step he doesn't stumble.

Kris deflates, releasing the tension she's been holding since my gasp.

"Is Johnny here?" the boy asks, but before Dan or I have the chance to answer a door bangs and Jonathan emerges from around the side of the house.

He's hurrying towards the barn with his head down, no doubt on his way to start the afternoon's work.

I wonder if he's taken over all the horse stuff, or if Beth has managed to find someone else to help.

My chest closes up at the sight of him in his stupid new work boots, worn out jeans and faded grey shirt.

I glance at Dan and he's already moving towards me. He rests a reassuring hand on my back. It's warm and solid and safe, but I still feel a little like I'm going to be sick.

Jonathan is almost even with us now, where we stand slightly to the side of his direct route to the barn.

Kris bounds over to him.

"Johnny!" she cries and envelopes him in a hug. He startles, but hugs her back briefly as she whispers something to him before she pushes him away. "I'm going to meet my cousin."

Then she skips off towards the house.

The boy on crutches hasn't said a word. He watches in silence as Jonathan gets closer, his gaze following his sister's path to the house. He still hasn't seen us.

He finally glances in our direction and recoils violently. He's staring directly at me.

"Hollie," he says, his voice deep, and my heart twists at the way he says my name. "What're you doing here?" He bites out the question, then notices I'm not alone.

He's not looking at me anymore.

He's dismissed me already with his scathing question.

I was right.

He doesn't want me here and I don't even have the chance to apologise – not that I'd be able to get the words out.

He takes a few steps towards us, staring at the boy.

Jonathan's face has gone as pale as I've ever seen it.

His hand is tangled up in his hair again, a sure sign of distress. He looks like he might pass out right there in the driveway.

I'm surprised by the pang of sympathy that edges past all the pain I'm feeling.

I want to go over to him and wrap him in a hug, like I did a week ago at the party. I want to be able to hug the pain right out of him.

I've wondered about it a lot this week, this thing that hurts him so badly and how I could have helped him.

But I can't go over there now … because he hates me.

The boy, whose identity is sitting right below the surface of my conscious thought, takes a few laboured steps forward. Nobody else moves.

Then it comes to me like a bolt of lightning.

The photograph I've seen of him.

He's different in so many ways. His hair is short now, his face sharper like he's lost a lot of weight, and the grim, pained look etched into his features is a stark contrast to the relaxed, wide grin in the photo.

I know exactly who this is.

Jonathan confirms it for me with a single word, his voice strangled and broken.

"Luke."

CHAPTER 27

Jonathan

"LUKE."

I manage to get the single word out, but others I might say in this situation are stuck in my throat.

I thought the shock of seeing Mum standing in Beth's kitchen as I stumbled down the stairs was the worst I'd get for today. As soon as she caught sight of me she pulled me into a rib-crushing hug.

I was speechless.

I hugged her back, because as much as a teenage boy shouldn't miss his mum, I still do, and it was so nice to see her again.

"I've missed you so much," she whispered against my hair, before eventually releasing her grip and holding me at arm's length, studying me.

I couldn't look her in the eye. I tried, but couldn't do it.

She opened her mouth to speak, but before she had the chance to say anything I blurted out that I needed to get to work and bolted for the door.

She's here to take me home.

I know it.

Beth hasn't said as much, because I've been avoiding her again, but I know.

She doesn't want me here – not when I'm such a liability.

So, I ran for the door, banging it shut behind me.

Once outside I was accosted by Kristen.

Another bone-pulverising hug.

Another "I've missed you" whispered into my hair before she raced inside to meet Thea.

I watched her go, using her whirlwind of energy as a distraction from my emotions.

I've missed her too, even if she is my little sister.

One more person I've abandoned in my selfish attempt to escape reality. Which, of course, hasn't worked – and I managed to hurt even more people.

I was just starting to get my emotions and my breathing under control when I looked up and my eyes landed on Hollie.

Hollie.

She looked a mess. She's still beautiful – I don't think she'll ever not be beautiful – but she looked exhausted.

Her face was pale, emphasising the freckles across her cheeks and the dark circles under her eyes. Her hair was scraped back into a rough ponytail.

Then, there was the cast. I tried not to look at it, or the crutches she was leaning on.

"What are you doing here?" I said, still in shock, my voice coming out harsher than I intended.

So many shocks, one after the other. It's leaving me off balance.

But neither Mum nor Kristen nor Hollie is the biggest shock.

The biggest shock is Luke.

Luke standing in front of me.

Standing.

He's staring back at me, his face stony.

He looks the same, but also so different. Everything about him feels sharper and more severe.

He's lost weight. What used to be toned muscle has faded. It hasn't gone soft; it's just gone, leaving him looking too skinny for his frame.

I can see it in his face, too. It's harsher now.

Or maybe that's bitterness from his best friend's betrayal.

His hair is short. I blink and do a double take. I've never, ever seen his hair short.

"You cut your hair."

The words tumble out before I have the chance to notice how utterly stupid they are. I haven't seen my best friend in three months – since I did this to him – and *this* is what I say?

Luke looks as unimpressed with me as I feel. "They had to shave half of it for the stitches," he says, his voice wary and guarded.

I'm distracted by the sound of an engine, and I realise Hollie is back in Dan's car and he's slowly reversing away from the fence.

"Hang on," I gasp at Luke and run for the car.

Hollie can't leave, not before I have the chance to apologise. If Mum is taking me home today I won't have another chance.

I don't expect her to forgive me, but I still have to say the words, if only for my own selfish reasons.

I knock on the passenger side window as Dan stops to put

the car into forward gear. Hollie glances up at me through the glass, then shakes her head.

I knock again, harder this time, banging my fist against the glass. "Please open the window," I say, hopefully loud enough for her to hear me.

I see her sigh – the way her body moves gives it away – but the window slowly creeps down.

"Hollie," I begin.

"Don't," she cuts me off. Up close she looks even worse, her eyes bloodshot and skin sallow. "I'm really sorry, okay? I'll leave you alone. I won't be back." Then she turns to Dan. "Let's go."

"But Hollie," Dan says, his voice calm.

"GO!" Hollie shouts at him, and I stumble back a step.

I've never heard her yell. I couldn't have even imagined her speaking with such hate in her voice.

I know the hatred isn't for Dan, even though he caught the brunt of it.

"Wait," I say, pleading, stepping forward again, placing my hand on the car door.

"No!" Hollie yells at me this time. "Drive, Dan, just *drive*."

And he does.

With a pitying glance at me, he presses down on the accelerator and the car pulls away, building speed and leaving a cloud of gravel dust in its wake.

I watch until it disappears from view, something inside me splintering, then turn back to Luke.

He's been watching the whole scene with the same emotionless look on his face.

Mum and Kris are inside with Beth and Thea.

Hollie and Dan are gone.

It's me and Luke standing in the driveway, staring at each other.

I'm literally facing the consequences of my actions.

I have no idea what I'm supposed to say.

"Was she the one driving your car?" Luke breaks the silence stretching between us.

I nod.

Luke was virtually part of my family, so I have no doubt either my parents or my sister told him what had happened, not realising he no longer wants anything to do with me.

"How bad is it?" he asks, voice still steely.

"Write-off," I say. "Chassis is bent." I tilt my head towards the vehicle trailer hooked up behind Mum's SUV. "I'm guessing that's what the trailer's for."

It's Luke's turn to nod.

The silence stretches out again.

"Why're you here?" I finally say.

He's silent for another moment, watching me, and I shift my weight. Heaviness hangs in the air between us, filled with pain and regret.

I'm not sure I'm ready to hear this. I'm not sure I'll ever be ready.

"There's something I need to say to you, but you wouldn't answer when I tried to call. When Kris said they were coming here I convinced them to bring me."

He's angry.

Obviously.

Why wouldn't he be?

Of course he is.

He's managing to keep a lid on it for now, though. Like any athlete, he has a strong helping of passion, and I know it often comes out of Luke in little bursts of anger. He's not aggressive or violent; he just needs to get it out sometimes.

He turns away abruptly and starts slowly — awkwardly — walking towards the fence, where the three horses are lined up. They're probably wondering why they're missing out on all their usual attention, but I'm staring after Luke, watching as he *walks*.

It's not something I thought I'd ever see again.

Not knowing what else to do, I fall into slow step beside Luke.

"She's not your girlfriend?"

"What?" I look up at Luke. I've been studying the careful way he now walks, cautiously placing each foot before transitioning weight to it.

"The girl." He tilts his head, indicating where Dan and Hollie drove away. "The one who was driving your car?" He says all this like it's obvious, but it's such an unexpected question, it's taking a moment for my brain to catch up.

"No," I say, wishing I was lying. "In case you couldn't tell from before, she hates me." Even though I've been thinking it for a week, it still hurts to say the words out loud.

"But you don't hate her." He knows me too well, there's no use denying it.

"No. Never, but it's not like that matters."

"Is that guy her boyfriend?" Wow, he's really into kicking me while I'm down.

"No, he's just her friend, but like I said, it doesn't matter."

"So, what'd you do to make her hate you?" He's smirking down at me and it hits me how damn much I've missed having him around. He's always thought he's so funny.

He actually is, but I'm also really, really over the inquisition.

"Shit, man," I say as I turn to face him. "Did you come all this fucking way to harass me about a girl who hates me and is likely never going to speak to me again? You gonna rub it in a little more?"

"Dude," he says, placatingly. "I was having you on. Didn't realise it was such a touchy subject. Sorry."

I exhale. I don't know where I stand with him. I don't know why he's ribbing me. This is not at all how I expected seeing him again would play out.

"Right, well," I say. "Can you let me have it? I've got shit to do."

"Let you have it?"

"Yeah. You said you had things you needed to say. Let me have it, then."

"Geez," he says, scowling. "No wonder she doesn't want to have anything to do with you. Cranky bastard."

I bristle and glare at him. He rolls his eyes and leans on the fence.

A warm nose pushes over my shoulder and huffs hot air into my face.

"Gross, Harley," I say, gently pushing him away but giving him a scratch under his chin as I do. He relaxes under my touch and it's strangely soothing. Maybe I'm starting to understand why Hollie enjoys these guys so much.

I glance at Luke out of the corner of my eye. Alaska's sniffing at him, but he ignores her while continuing to stare at me.

I sigh, a long, defeated exhale.

I'm not getting out of this and he's not going to make it easy for me. Not that he should.

"I fucked it up, all right? We had a moment, I screwed it up, that's when she had the accident…" I trail off. I hate thinking about that night.

"How'd you screw it up?"

I turn on him, pressure building behind my eyes, tension rising in my body. "I just *did*. Does it really even matter? I hurt her and she got in that accident because of it." I lean into Harley's neck and he nibbles on my shirt.

Seeing Luke again is … not what I expected. And actually, I didn't expect to see him again at all – or at least not for a really long time.

Definitely not right when my life has turned to complete shit again.

I wish that things could go back to the way they used to be. But they can't.

I'm on edge, waiting for the moment when Luke veers from this strange calmness and mild exasperation with me into the anger that must be simmering below the surface.

"You know you can apologise to people when you hurt them?"

There it is.

The reason he's here. Not that it'll change anything.

Saying a few words isn't going to fix anything, even if I mean them more than anything else I'll ever say in my life.

"You should really give it a go," Luke continues. "You might be lucky; she might talk to you again."

"I've *tried*! I've tried to apologise, but it was my fault. The accident was my fault and she's never going to forgive me for it." My voice breaks and I turn away before Luke can see the tears that abruptly fill my vision. I dash my hand across my eyes, wiping away the moisture.

"I don't understand how the accident was your fault," Luke says, voice sliding from exasperation to frustration.

"Haven't you been listening to anything I said?" I'm on the verge of shouting.

Harley shies and tosses his head at the sudden change in volume, and I reach out to settle him with a soothing hand.

Luke doesn't say anything so I carry on talking, dropping my voice low. "She was in that car because of me. It was my fault. If it weren't for me, she'd never have been in that accident."

"Dude!" Luke's voice matches mine. "You weren't the drunk-ass driver that ploughed through an intersection, were you? It wasn't your fault! It wasn't her fault either, and she's the one who got in the car. The only one at fault here is the loser who drove after drinking and smashed into her. Saying her accident was your fault is like saying mine was your fault too!"

The world stops as his words hit my consciousness.

We've made it to why Luke came four hours to see me. Why, after all these months, he wants to see me again.

My breath lodges in my throat and my lungs are a vacuum. I can't catch a breath. There's no oxygen anywhere.

The world shifts and tilts, the edges blurring.

I'm not entirely sure I know which way is up.

There's a sharp pain in my shoulder.

"Johnny!" Luke's poked me with the end of one of his crutches. "Johnny, are you okay?"

The tiniest breath comes.

A sip of air.

Then another one, and another.

Harley pushes against my shoulder. I focus on that warm, horsey smell, that should be awful but isn't. It reminds me of Hollie.

Luke prods me again. "You okay, man?"

I take stock of myself.

My breathing has resumed.

My heart is still racing, but it's manageable.

I nod.

Luke's sizing me up and I brace myself for whatever he's going to say next. I grip the fence, the timber railing rough against my palms and fingertips.

"Since when do you have panic attacks?"

Panic attacks.

I'm having panic attacks?

The realisation hits me like a blow.

The party.

Thea's bedroom with Hollie that day.

Countless other times when I thought I was dying, but didn't.

"December," I whisper, my voice scratchy and hoarse.

"Because of this?" Luke gestures to himself, and I nod.

"I'm really, really sorry. You'll never know how much," I blurt out. The tears are back, making my eyes hot and everything a little hazy.

The words land in the space between us, right in the giant void that's been there since that night.

Since he made me swear not to tell anyone what happened. I promised I'd never tell a soul.

"You never came back." Now it's Luke's voice crackling over his words.

"I did," I say. "I came back and you never wanted to see

me. I got the picture pretty quick."

"You didn't stop coming because of what happened before I got hurt?" His voice is shaky and I can hear the anger in it.

Wait, no.

Not anger.

Fear.

"No! Of course not. Never," I say, not sure where this is even coming from.

"Then why the fuck did you abandon me?" There's so much anger in those words I want to run from them, but there's also so much pain, especially in the last two words.

"I didn't. I didn't abandon you," I say, my voice rising again. The anger is easier to bear than any other emotion that might want to break out right now.

Except obviously I did abandon him and I'm a complete coward.

They say the truth hurts.

Luke turns away from the fence where he's been leaning his weight.

The movement is slow and precise. Careful. He still winces with the motion. His face is like thunder and he glowers down at me.

"I broke my spine. Crushed two vertebrae. I lost the ability to walk and thought I never would again. It's been three months – *three* – and this is the first time I've seen you since the day after it happened. What kind of asshole are you to leave? Not even a phone call to say you were leaving town. Not even a text!"

"You didn't want to see me, remember?" I shout back at him.

The three horses throw their heads up and skitter away

from us. I should care that we're upsetting them, but I'm over-whelmed with hurt and rage. It's burning through my limbs, constricting my chest.

"I came back to see you, over and over, and you *never* wanted to see me. Every time I came it was, 'Oh, he's sleeping,' 'He's having tests,' or plain old 'He doesn't want to see you.'" I take a few gasping breaths. "What was I supposed to do? Break into your hospital room and take you hostage? You didn't want to see me!"

I can't be here anymore.

I can't be standing here having a conversation with him.

All I've wanted for months is to be with him again.

But things will never, ever be the same.

I'll never get past this and he shouldn't have to.

I exhale as much of the anger as I can. "I'm really, truly sorry. You'll never know how fucking sorry I am that I did this to you, that I left and that I didn't *make* you see me, so I could tell you how sorry I was – over and over. But you didn't want to see me, and I was trying to make it easier for you and obviously I was wrong, and I'm sorry about that too."

"I only wanted a little bit of time. I needed some time to process everything. Why the fuck would I never want to see you again? And why do you keep apologising?"

"Because you know as well as I do that this was my fault. Like with Hollie, *this was my fault!*" I gesture wildly at him, encompassing the crutches and the way he moves now.

Then, because I'm a terrible, awful human, I spin on my heel and march away from him, knowing full well he can't follow me.

Because he can hardly walk.

Because of what I did.

CHAPTER 28

Hollie

DAN IS quiet the whole way home.

He doesn't try to make me go anywhere else.

He shuts up and drives.

For that I am grateful, even if I'm absolutely seething with anger at him for taking me to Beth's in the first place, knowing Jonathan would be there too.

And I was stupid enough to go along with it, so I'm angry at myself too.

Because I didn't think it would be this bad.

But it is this bad.

The way he looked at me with his eyes trailing down me.

Any of the nice memories I'd ever had of him – riding in the hills, dancing in Beth's kitchen, every subtle touch, the kissing – are all erased because of that look and the way his voice curled as he spoke.

What are you doing here?

I can't believe I let Dan talk me into going there.

Dan pulls into my driveway and turns off the car.

I grab my crutches, which I've kept in the front seat with me this time, and begin to haul myself out of the car.

Dan appears at my door, but I ignore his touch on my arm and ignore him further when he offers me his hand.

I clomp up the path to my front door and I can tell Dan is following me. I shove my key into the lock and twist. I'm surprised it goes in on my first attempt. My hands are shaking with emotion.

"Hollie." Dan touches my arm again and I pause, staring down at his tanned hands against my skin. "I'm sorry," he says, "that's not how I thought it would go."

"And how exactly did you expect it to go?" I whirl around. Well, I whirl as much as anyone can while on crutches. "What did you expect to happen? That he'd smile and make a joke and everything would be fine? Nothing is fine, Daniel."

He flinches at my use of his full name, at the anger in my voice.

"Maybe if he'd had a chance to explain…"

"It wouldn't make a difference. It doesn't matter. He's not the problem. I'm the problem!"

My brain is making irrational leaps.

Somewhere in the bottom of my consciousness I know I'm making irrational leaps, but they keep happening.

"I should never have gone there," I yell. "He doesn't want to see me and I threw it right in his face."

"I'm not sure that's right, Hollie," Dan says, voice still calm. "I think he wanted to talk to you."

"No, he didn't. But it doesn't matter. None of it matters. Go home, Dan, and leave me alone."

"Holls." He's reaching out for me again but I shove him back, stumbling a little.

"No. Go away, Dan. I know you feel sorry for me. I know that's why you're here. You want to fix me. But I'm unfixable, all right? I'm broken. Beyond repair." I stop for a breath, panting.

"You're not broken, Hollie."

"I am!" I shout, despite him keeping his voice low and calm. "Give it up. Kait hates me, Jonathan hates me. There's something wrong in my head. I can't keep doing this. Stop pretending I'm normal. I'll never be normal and you'll never be able to fix me!"

I finish my tirade and limp over the threshold. Dan is standing on the other side, face stricken. He goes to move forward, but before he gets the chance to say anything I slam the door in his face.

The sound releases the sobs and I slide to the floor, body writhing as the pain consumes me.

"Hollie!"

There's banging somewhere above me.

Dan.

He's knocking on the door. It automatically locks, so he needs a key, or someone to open it from the inside, to get in. My keys are in my hand, the sharp points digging into my palm.

"Go away!" I shriek.

"No." His voice is resolute. "I'm not leaving you here like this, Hollie."

"I don't want you here!"

"I don't care, Hollie. Because this isn't you…"

"It *is* me," I shout as more sobs course through me, tears dripping down my face, vision blurred, anger and pain pulsing at my temples.

"It's not the real you, Hollie. I'm not leaving you alone right now."

I slide further until I'm lying on the floor.

I can't argue with him anymore.

It's too hard to arrange my thoughts into words.

So I simply lie on the front hallway floor, crying until I'm exhausted.

All the thoughts turn over in my head, swirling around in this dark, bleak vortex.

How useless I am.

How much I've failed.

How I've let everyone down.

Each thought is like a knife through my heart.

My head is throbbing in time with every pained heartbeat.

I can't take it.

I can't do this anymore.

The pain's too much.

It's too constant.

Every time I have a glimpse of something else, of my life being more than counselling and forcing myself to go for runs so I can function like the bare minimum of a normal person, I fall again.

All that work – months of work, of fighting every single day to get myself out of bed, to go to school, to work, to have friends, just fighting to function.

And it's gone again.

It was all for nothing.

This is my life now.

Episode after episode of failing, of not being able to get better.

I can't take it.

CHAPTER 29

Jonathan

FIVE MONTHS AGO

IT'S dark when I step outside onto the footpath.

The December air is warm and humid, but it's still refreshing after being surrounded by a crush of sweaty bodies drinking and dancing and making out.

It must have been raining earlier, because the footpath is dark and slick under my sneakers. Streetlights glow above me, but they're losing a battle against the brightly lit restaurants, bars and clubs lining this street.

I pause under the light of one and pull out my phone. The pinkish glow of a club's sign throws a weird hue over the screen and turns my hands a strange colour. I swipe open the ongoing chat with Luke and Kristen, unable to delay it any longer.

I've spent the evening at a bar, checking out their music set-up and convincing the manager that she wants both to employ me, and to have our band play there sometimes.

I was successful on both counts, and a grin spreads across my face as I start typing.

Then I stop and delete the message.

Sometimes you don't want to share your best news with your little sister first.

I tap directly into Luke's details and swipe across the screen to start a call. I put the phone to my ear and start walking again, heading for my car that's parked around the corner.

I pause when I glance up and catch sight of two people on the balcony used to access the club with the pink sign. It's set back from the street, a narrow staircase leading up to the entrance.

The two figures are standing a little way further down the deck, away from the door, in a dimly lit corner. There's light somewhere behind them, probably another neon bar sign, that casts them in silhouette. It's shadowy enough that I can't make out their faces, but by their size and build I'm picking it's two guys sharing a quiet moment.

The shorter one, with hair spiked up and glowing slightly blue from the back lighting, reaches up and runs a hand along the other's cheek. He pushes the other guy's hair back from his face, then stretches up and presses their lips together.

There's a moment where they break apart, as if the one who made the move is waiting for permission from the other to continue. Then the taller guy leans forward to continue the kiss, deepening it.

The caution evaporates fast, passion flaring between them. Their hands explore, tangling in each other's clothes and hair.

I stand there frozen with my phone to my ear, listening to it ring as I watch them. I sort of wish I'd never noticed them.

Not because I care what they're doing or who they are, but because I feel like I'm intruding.

Also, it's making me wish I had someone I could make out with in the neon glow of a sign.

They break apart as the taller guy reaches into his pocket, pulls out a phone, taps the screen and shoves it back into his pocket before resuming the kissing.

I sigh and turn away as Luke's voice comes through my phone speaker.

His answerphone.

I can't believe he blew me off tonight, though I guess he didn't really have a choice if his parents insisted on a family dinner.

But he would have loved this bar.

Since neither of us is eighteen yet, it's a novel experience being allowed inside a bar, and we usually make the most of it. Obviously, we aren't allowed near the actual bar, only near the sound equipment and stage when we're playing, but it's still an experience that hasn't grown old.

Tonight was the first time I've had to score us a venue alone. We always do it together, and I'm not sure if I'm imagining things or if there's been a subtle shift in our relationship recently that would explain Luke's unease when I told him about going to scope out this venue tonight.

He just doesn't seem as invested in this whole music thing as he was six months ago, or maybe it's just that he's never been as into it as me.

It shouldn't surprise me. He probably wants to travel once we finish school. He probably wants to take his mountain bike and disappear to Europe, and when he comes home he'll probably be a world champion.

Maybe he's realised that's what he really wants to do but he doesn't know how to tell me, because music is all I've ever wanted to do.

I push all these thoughts away. We'll deal with all that someday, but right now I want to tell him about my new job.

I swipe at my phone again and dial Luke's number again. I start walking, and by the time the phone is ringing I've drawn alongside the couple still on the balcony slightly above me.

"Your phone again," one of them says, breaking off the kiss.

The other groans. I can't see them properly anymore, but I assume he's pulling his phone out of his pocket again.

"Johnny, huh? Should I be worried?" It's the first guy again.

"Nah, just my friend. He'll leave us alone soon."

"Good. I was hoping you'd want to get out of here."

"Sounds good to me."

I'm frozen on the footpath.

My phone is pressed against my ear as I listen again to Luke's voicemail message.

The beep sounds.

I don't leave a message.

What did I just hear?

My name.

A voice I didn't recognise … but one that I did.

Sort of. It doesn't sound quite right, but I'd know that voice anywhere.

I turn and take a few backward steps towards the street, watching as the couple comes into view.

They're harder to see in this light, but now I know what I'm looking for, it's obvious.

It's Luke.

What.

The.

Hell.

My foot slips off the edge of the curb and I swear, but manage to catch myself before I fall.

I glance up at Luke and the other guy. They've broken apart and are both facing me, gripping each other's arms. With the light behind them I still can't see their faces, but I can feel the glow on my own face, so I know they can see me clearly.

Luke jerks away from the other guy.

I take the stairs two at a time. They're slippery, and so is the decking. I slide to a stop in front of my best friend.

He says nothing, just staring at me in shock and horror. There may be a little bit of fear under there, too. He's swaying slightly and I wonder if he's been drinking.

"What the hell, Luke?" I say, surprised how calm my voice sounds. Inside my head is not calm at all, with dozens of thoughts crashing into one another as I try to process them all.

His flight or fight response must kick in. He goes for flight, but before he can get past me I grab hold of him, pulling him to a stop. "Luke, wait."

He grabs at his hair and tugs at the ends. He groans. "This cannot be happening."

"Luke, hey, take a breath, stop a second." I've got him by both shoulders, holding him firmly in place, stopping him turning away from me.

One hand covers his face, the other yanking his hair. It's long, sitting barely above his shoulders in a dark curtain. Many girls over the years have complained how jealous they are of his hair.

But now his fingers clutch at the ends and he's tearing at it.

Tugging the ends has always been a bit of a nervous tic for him, but this is a whole new level. He'll start ripping it out if he carries on.

His whole body is tense and shaking, still trying to escape my grasp.

"Luke, look at me."

He slowly lifts his gaze. His face is inches from mine and his eyes are wild, glassy with emotion. He's breathing hard.

"Luke, it's okay."

He shakes his head, trying to push me off him again. But we've been wrestling – play-fighting – since we were six years old, and I know his limits. I hold firm.

"Not. Not okay," he gasps. "I don't … I don't want people to know. Don't want you to know."

This last bit hurts, like a shaft of ice through my heart.

Does he really think I won't be okay with this? I guess it's not something we've ever talked about, but I hope I don't come across as the sort of person who'd have an issue with his best friend being gay, or bi, or whatever he is. He's still Luke – will always be Luke. Who he wants to kiss is never going to change that.

He's muttering between gasps of breath, and I can only make out a few words. "Not ready … don't even know … changes everything."

"Luke," I say, squeezing his shoulders hard. "Stop, Luke."

He stops. He looks at me.

After a moment he shrugs my hands off his shoulders and I let them fall away. He takes deep breaths, calming down.

"Nothing needs to change, Luke," I say when I think he can cope with conversation again.

"It will. Everything will be different. You'll be different," he says, finally looking me in the eye.

"No, I won't."

"Then why'd you charge up here swearing at me?"

"Because I want to know why you lied to me and what the hell you're thinking sneaking out, getting into a club and agreeing to go home with some random guy."

He blinks at me, then glances at the other guy, who hasn't moved.

"You wouldn't get it, Johnny," he says, and his voice is tired. He holds out a hand to the other guy. "We still getting out of here?"

The guy glances between Luke and me. "You sure this isn't something you need to sort out?"

Luke shakes his head. "No. Johnny will get over it." He turns to me. "You tell anyone and I swear we're done. For good."

My mouth opens, then closes. He sounds so calm, but also, he can't quite form his words correctly. I don't know how to deal with that last threat, so I say the only thing I can.

"Luke, there's no way in hell I am letting you leave with this guy."

"It's not your call," he snaps back.

"How do you know him?" I ask, and my question seems to take him by surprise. I follow it up quickly. "Did you meet him tonight or do you know him from somewhere else?"

Now it's his turn to look like a goldfish, with his mouth opening and closing, trying to find the right words.

"Does it really matter?" the other guy drawls. "He's allowed to have a little fun, you know. You don't have to be jealous."

Oh, I want to hit him so bad. I really don't think that's going to help my case with Luke, though.

"You met him tonight, yeah?" I ignore the other guy and focus on Luke.

He nods, but in a way that lets me know he really, really wishes I wasn't right. His eyes are burning into mine, like he knows what I'm going to say next and he's willing me not to.

"Does he know how old you are?"

Luke's chin twitches to the side.

The other guy scoffs. "It doesn't matter. We're all adults here. There's nothing wrong with having a good time."

I turn on him then, unable to take his condescending bullshit anymore. "Sure, absolutely nothing wrong with having a good time. I'm totally for that. Usually I wouldn't care who my friend was spending time with, except when that person is … how old, exactly?"

"Twenty-four," he says with a shrug. "So what?" But I've taken the edge of his attitude and he's looking sideways at Luke.

"Mmhmm, yeah. I'm totally for my friend having a good time, but you know, would prefer it was with guys a little closer in age."

"What?" The guy is openly staring at Luke now. Meanwhile, Luke has closed his eyes and is biting down on his lips, hands clenched at his side.

I hate to be doing this. I really don't want to hurt Luke, but I don't know how I can get him out of this situation any other way. He won't back down. I need the other guy to walk away.

I sigh. Maybe I should never have got involved.

But would a sober Luke really want to go home with a guy

seven years older than him? Will he wake up in the morning and regret it?

At least I'm giving him the option to make the choice sober on another day. Probably not with this guy, mind you, but he's a bit of a dick, so maybe sober Luke will thank me for that too.

"Are you going to tell him or am I?" I ask Luke.

He says nothing, just opens his eyes and glares at me.

I sigh again. "He's seventeen," I say, and the guy blinks in shock, then backs up a step.

Luke goes after him. "I'm sorry," he says, reaching for his arm. "I didn't lie to you. I didn't think it mattered that much."

"Yeah, it matters," he says, looking Luke up and down before turning to me. "You'd better take him home." He takes another step away from Luke, then slides sideways and disappears through the doorway to the club.

Luke whirls on me. "I cannot believe you just did that."

"Well, I can't believe you blew me off, lied to me, got drunk and tried to go home with some random dude!"

He makes an aggravated sound and spins away from me, heading back towards the entrance to the club.

I grab his arm.

"No way. You're coming home."

"I'm not going anywhere with you," he says and shoves me.

My shoes lose their grip on the slippery decking, and I step quickly backwards, trying to catch myself before I fall on my ass.

Luke's eyes widen in shock and he comes after me, trying to grab my hand and stop me going down.

My back hits against the railing and we both stumble with the abrupt shift in momentum. Luke crashes into me and I shove him away.

It should be nothing. A shove where Luke takes one step to absorb the movement and correct himself.

But instead of one step, he takes two, and in a blur his foot goes off the edge of the first step.

Someone screams.

It sounds suspiciously like me.

Then Luke is at the bottom of the steps, sprawled on the footpath in a puddle of light from the streetlight above.

He isn't moving at all.

I fly down the stairs, not feeling my feet connect with them.

I shove a dark shadow out of the way as I drop to my knees beside the crumpled form of my best friend. It must have been someone on the street who saw him fall.

"Hey," the person says, indignant.

But I ignore them.

Whoever it is, they don't know Luke.

Not like I know him.

There is blood on the side of his face already, along his temple. I touch it lightly, feeling the damp warmth on my fingertips.

A hand rests on my shoulder. "Hey, mate, don't touch him. You could make it worse. We'll get some help."

But that is all I want to do – touch him, shake him, make him wake up.

He stirs and mumbles something unintelligible, his eyes flickering. Then he goes still again.

A crowd has gathered; people from the street or nearby restaurants and bars.

"Oh my god, oh my god, oh my god," a girl behind me is gasping. Someone beside her is sobbing. Someone else is on the phone.

"Ambulance," she says.

Red lights are flashing, and I'm dragged back and pulled away from Luke. His hair is thick with blood now, his face pale and his body still motionless.

Paramedics fasten a brace around his neck, strap him to a board.

I'm being held upright by a group of strangers. I don't know who they are but they support me so my knees don't buckle and leave me a crumpled mess on the ground beside Luke.

When the paramedics start asking questions, everyone directs them to me.

The woman beside me rests a gentle hand on my shoulder and encourages me to tell them what they need to know.

I reel off Luke's name, his age, that I think he's been drinking but don't really know, that I'm pretty sure he doesn't have any allergies, that someone needs to call his mum.

They thank me for the information and ask if I want to go with him. The woman squeezes my shoulder again then wraps me in a hug, telling me that everything is going to be okay.

I don't believe her at all, and without another word follow Luke into the ambulance.

CHAPTER 30

Jonathan

"JOHNNY."

Luke's voice is low, drifting up to me where I've hidden in the back of the barn. There's a loft thing that Beth uses for storage, and it's where I headed after walking away from Luke.

I hauled myself up the ladder and flopped onto the dusty wooden floor.

Something tickled my face and I swiped at it, surprised to find my fingers wet.

I'd got my apology out.

Unfortunately, I'd shouted it at him.

But I'd said the words.

The anger I'd felt – that he'd ignited in me – faded away and I was left hollow, the tears leaving wavering tracks down my face.

I lay in the dim dusty barn and finally let the memories come.

I didn't push them down or fight them back to the darkest corners of my brain.

I let them come and remind me exactly what I'd done.

It didn't matter which way I looked at it, I was responsible for Luke tumbling down those stairs.

I didn't need to get all up in his face about what he was doing. I didn't need to let my temper get the better of me.

I should have let it go and let Luke tell me whatever he needed to when he was ready.

I shouldn't have been all self-righteous, thinking I knew better and that he needed protecting.

I sigh at his voice now, and peer down through the railings. Luke looks exhausted as he glances around the barn, trying to figure out where I am.

"Johnny, what'd you mean?"

I push myself upright and slide to the ladder.

He won't give up.

It's his nature. It's that damn tenacity that probably got him walking again. I swing down.

"You look like you need to sit down," I mutter.

I don't want to have this conversation. He needs to go. I've said sorry. I don't know what else he wants.

"What did you mean? Why is it your fault?" That steely edge is back in his voice and I know I'm not getting out of this. Though he really, really does look like he needs to sit down.

"Because of what I did!"

"What did you do?" He's looking completely blank, and a realisation hits me.

"What do you remember?"

He stares at me and I can see him thinking, trying to fill in the missing pieces. "I remember the club, and a guy, and you seeing me on that balcony. I remember freaking out. Then the hospital."

"You don't remember the fall?"

He shakes his head.

"Or what happened before you fell?"

He shakes his head again.

"I thought you'd remembered. But…" I cover my mouth with my hands. I knew that the day after the accident he'd had no recollection of what had happened, but then I assumed his memory had come back, and that's why he didn't want to see me. "You don't remember our fight?"

His face goes white – in a blink all the colour is gone – and he staggers, like his knees have gone weak. He manages to hold himself up, but barely.

"We were fighting?" he asks in a whisper. "Did you—"

"No!" I shout, cutting him off. But I did. "I … It wasn't on purpose," I whisper. "You didn't just slip going down the stairs as you were leaving."

My hand has found its way to my hair. Again, I think of Hollie and the smart-ass grin she gave as she mocked me for it.

I feel my voice catch in my throat, but I force more words out.

"You know I saw you, and you were pretty panicked. I tried to calm you down, then you tried to leave with that guy. You were going to go home with him and I didn't think you should," I say, my voice coming out as a hoarse whisper.

Luke doesn't say anything, so I continue.

"I tried to stop you." I'm shaking all over and slide down the wall to sit on the floor. "I was such an ass to you, Luke. You didn't want to leave with me and I made this huge drama about how old you were in front of the other guy."

I drop my head into my hands and pull my legs into my chest. My head rests against my knees and I haul in some deep breaths, trying to steady myself again. There's too much emotion, and after a week of constant heightened emotion it's almost too much to bear.

"You were so mad at me. I knew what I was doing and I did it anyway. I pissed you off so much that you pushed me. I slipped, you tried to catch me, and we stumbled. I pushed you off me. Then you went over the edge, and next minute you were at the bottom of those steps."

"I still don't see how this is your fault," Luke says, eventually.

"Because I'm the reason for all of it! I'm why you fell and why you got hurt. Because I had to argue with you. I couldn't leave shit alone and let you come to me when you were ready. I had to push and push and not let you just figure shit out on your own. If I'd shut my mouth it wouldn't have happened."

"Because you didn't want me being with a guy?"

"Because I didn't want you going home with some random guy you didn't even know. I don't care that you're gay, Luke. I don't."

"But you *do* care," he cries out. "I remember your face when you saw me up on that balcony, with him. I saw the look on your face. I see it every single day now. Every time I think about you, that's all I can see!"

"Whatever look was on my face was nothing to do with you kissing a guy! It was because you'd ditched me and lied to me. God, I was pissed about that." I'm twisted up with anguish remembering that night over and over. "I didn't care Luke! I don't care!"

"Then why did you leave?" He has tears on his face when I peer up at him, his voice twisted and wrecked.

"Because," I say quietly, "you blamed me for the accident. Because it was my fault."

"No I didn't! I don't remember anything, only the disgusted look on your face when you saw me!"

"But I *wasn't* disgusted! Whatever you saw was me being angry and confused because you lied about having dinner with your parents, or – I dunno – it's just my face. I don't care. Please believe me." There's anguish in my voice now too. "I love you, regardless of who you wanna date. It nearly killed me that you thought I'd be any different around you because of it. I thought you knew me better than that."

"I thought I did, too. I thought that once there was something to tell you, I would. But then you caught me out. And I wasn't ready for it. I didn't know what was happening or what I was doing."

"But you don't remember after, when I told you I didn't care? That it was okay? That I was happy for you?"

He shakes his head. He's found a spot to lean against the wall. He looks utterly broken, physically, emotionally, everything.

"No," he whispers. "I only remember your face. Then you wouldn't visit. You wouldn't visit because you hated me … for who I was."

"Never," I whisper back. "I thought you hated me for causing all this. For you getting hurt."

"Never," he tosses my words back at me, and for the first time in months I feel a glimmer of hope. "I was scared. You kept trying to talk to me about it, but I didn't want to talk about it, not even with you."

"Why not?" I ask, genuinely curious now. Luke lets out a sigh.

"Because you would have had questions – questions I wasn't ready to answer. I wasn't ready. You wanted me to tell someone. I needed some time, but you never came back."

"I meant we should tell someone what really happened. That you didn't just slip. The doctors couldn't figure out how you could just slip going down the stairs and wind up that injured, and your parents wanted to know why we were there … I needed to be able to talk to you first so I could be clear about what to tell them, so we had our stories straight… " I go quiet and think for a moment. "I never considered you'd think I wanted you to come out to all of them."

I climb to my feet and look at my friend. I take in his posture, the exhaustion and pain rolling off him. I pull down a hay bale from the stack at the back of the barn and heave it to where he's standing.

"I'm sorry," I say quietly, gesturing for him to sit. He takes my outstretched hand and uses it to lower himself onto the hay bale, grimacing as he does.

"You know a stupid argument and a couple of shoves don't make this your fault, right?" he says.

I plonk down on the opposite end of the hay bale and twist to face him. "If I'd shut my mouth, if I'd not been such a fucking self-righteous know-it-all, we wouldn't have had the stupid argument or the fight."

"Still not your fault," he says, a little smugly. "Come on, man, let it go."

"I can't," I say tightly, and get up from the bale.

"You gonna run away again, Johnny?"

I pause because yeah, I was going to run away again.

"Johnny, sometimes shit happens. You didn't push me. You

need to stop running and face it. My accident *was not your fault.*
It wasn't." He's sitting there so calmly after everything I've
told him.

"I've been a total asshole," I mutter, meaning not only to
him, but to my parents and sister, Beth, Hollie…

"Just because you've acted like one doesn't mean you are
one. Maybe you made a mistake, maybe I did. No, I definitely
did. But that one night doesn't determine who or what you are,
or who I am." He pauses, giving me a minute to process. "Did
you miss me?"

I turn to look at him again, expecting to see a smirk on his
face, but he's sitting there placidly, those damn crutches laid
down beside him, hands in his lap.

"Of course I did, but that doesn't make things right."

He shrugs. "You have to let it go, Johnny. You'll never move
forward if you don't."

"I don't know how," I whisper. All the things I've done, all
the people I've hurt, all because of that one night. "It's not that
one thing I did. It's months. Months of hurting people, over
and over. I don't know how to go back."

"Come here," he says, voice firm.

I take a couple of steps closer and realise he's trying to
stand up again. He mutters swear words under his breath. I
extend an arm and he grasps it. I help him to his feet.

Then he wraps his arm around me, using all the strength
he has to pull me in close. I slide my arms around him, taking
his weight. He's got a brace of some sort under his shirt. I can
feel the ridges beneath my palms. He leans in close to my ear.

"Stop running away. Stop blaming yourself, Johnny. If you
insist on bearing the blame, make it up to me by being my

friend again." He hugs me tight and I hug him back, way more gently. "And you know what? Stopping me from going home with some random guy I didn't know was a really, really good move."

Tears fill my eyes, but this time, for the first time in months, they're happy ones.

CHAPTER 31

Hollie

I'M NOT sure how long I lie on the floor of our front hallway.

Maybe I fall asleep; I don't really know.

Eventually my sobs subside, and the howling in my head calms a little.

I can hear someone talking.

It's Dan, I realise after a moment.

I try to make out another voice, to figure out who he's talking to, but there isn't one.

It's only Dan. His steady voice, low and calm, but loud enough that I can hear him through the door.

My head is clearing and I feel groggy and tired. I listen to what he's saying, trying to make sense of it.

And I realise he's talking about me.

He's telling me stories about myself. He's talking about the day we went bowling, the morning after I met Jonathan. He's talking about how smug I was when I won, how hard I laughed when we came up with the story behind his mum's party – the story about Great Aunt Kelsey and how she bequeathed them her house.

Then he starts talking about another day. We went to the beach, only the two of us, and I made him race me along the sand, showing off how fit I'd become with all the damned exercise I'd been doing to help improve my mental health.

Then, another day, when our friends were all together, well before my mental decline, and we spent the day eating fries and drinking milkshakes, and I remember sitting with Kait for hours and talking about anything and everything. I didn't think Dan even noticed me back then.

I lie on the cold tile floor listening to him talk. Through his stories, he tells me all the things he likes about me.

My stubbornness.

My laugh.

How completely in love with those horses I am.

He tells me all the good things; my kindness, generosity and loyalty, and eventually his words begin to sink in.

I force myself onto my knees and reach up for the door handle. I manage to twist it and unlatch the door, before sliding down to sit in a puddle on the floor again.

Dan pushes the door open. He's sitting leaning against the door frame, as if hanging out with a normal friend, not one who's had the most epic of meltdowns. He smiles at me across the hallway between us and holds out a hand. An invitation.

I crawl towards him, dragging my broken leg awkwardly behind me. I can't wait until they put it in a moon boot. He wraps his arm around me. I curl in, tucking my head under his chin.

"I'm sorry," I mutter, unable to look at him. I pick at some fraying denim on his jeans instead.

"Holls," he murmurs into my hair, pushing damp strands

away from my tear-stained face. "You have nothing to be sorry for. I know it's not your fault."

"I don't know what happens to me," I whisper. "It all gets so bad, like it builds up and then I explode. Then I feel like maybe things are bearable again."

"I know. I'd say it's all part of the depression."

I nod into his chest.

"Holls, maybe it's time to consider the pills? I know you said you didn't want them, but a lot's happened recently."

I nod again and let out a long breath.

"I thought I was better," I say, my breath hitching a little.

"Maybe it's not the type that's going to go away forever," he says carefully, and I shudder, holding in another sob. "I know that's scary, but you can fight this."

"I get so tired of fighting it. Why do I have to fight it all the time?"

"I don't know, Hollie, I really don't. But you can get through this." He pauses as his fingers untangle a knot in my hair. "You will do this, okay?"

I curl into him further, enjoying the way his fingers press into my scalp.

"Okay," I whisper. He seems so sure, maybe he's been right all along.

CHAPTER 32

Jonathan

I ROLL over and fall off the couch.

I hit the timber floor of Beth's lounge with a thud and a groan. I forgot where I was sleeping.

"You all right?" Luke's on the pull-out couch across the room. The stairs were too much for him last night, after the travelling and traipsing around after me while I had my tantrums.

So we slept here in the lounge. Kris is in my room and Mum's down the hall in Beth's guest room.

I grunt in response and haul myself up onto the couch again.

Luke's lying flat on his back, staring up at the ceiling, and I wonder how many ceilings he's got familiar with over the past few months.

We stayed up until the small hours of the night, catching up on everything we missed during our stupid misunderstanding.

I still feel the blame for the accident weighing heavily on

my shoulders, but Luke is adamant I have to let it go. Every time I got near an apology, or even referenced it, he shut me down.

He explained his injury and rehab in detail. I'd done my runner before the doctors had all the information, and I'd refused to let anyone tell me anything since. It's still a long road, but his prognosis is pretty good. They're not sure if he'll ever ride a bike again. When I asked him how he felt about that, he shrugged and said he'd already sold his bike.

Finally, long after Kris had gone to bed, I broached the subject we'd both been avoiding.

"So, will you tell me about that night?" I asked, after an extended lull in the conversation. He looked at me warily, but eventually nodded.

"It was my first time there," he said simply, without emotion. I'm not sure if he wanted to be talking about this or not.

"Why did you go?" I ventured, and Luke shrugged.

"There was this guy I kind of liked and I thought he'd be there."

I opened my mouth to ask, but Luke cut me off. "No, not that guy, another one. I was in an online forum thing and he was on there. He didn't know who I was though, and when I got there he was with someone else."

"Jerk," I muttered, and Luke gave me a dirty look. I opened my mouth to explain, but he beat me to it.

"We didn't have a relationship. We had chatted a couple of times online. He had no idea who I was. Until I went there that night and started dancing with that guy, no one in the real world knew. Except me, obviously."

I lay in the dark, listening to a cricket chirp outside. "Did you really think I wouldn't be okay with it?"

He gave an awkward shrug.

"I wasn't sure I was okay with it back then."

"Are you now?"

"I don't know. I haven't had much time for brooding over it. I wondered if it was just curiosity and then that one guy…" He trailed off. "But…"

"But what?"

"Nothing," he said.

"What? You can't start that and not finish," I demand.

He laughed softly, and a pang of longing went through me at the familiarity of it.

I stayed silent, hoping he was simply finding the words.

"Getting out of the car today," he says after an age, "my legs had a moment. I stumbled. It happens sometimes when I haven't used them in a while, like they've gone to sleep. That girl and her friend were there … he caught me, stopped me from falling. And … maybe it wasn't just curiosity and that one guy."

I sat up and stared across the darkness to where I could see him sprawled in the sofa bed.

"Dan?"

"Don't go there, Johnny," he said, voice sounding tired. "All I'm saying is that it probably wasn't only that one guy."

I lay back down, running through every interaction I'd had with Dan, any conversation I'd overheard about him, trying to figure out if I had any clue where his interests lay.

There was nothing.

I assumed he'd been dating Hollie, and hadn't considered anything further than that.

"All right," I said. "Regardless of whether it was 'just that one guy' as you keep saying, or something else, I'm going to be happy for you whatever, okay?"

"Okay," he said into the darkness, the trace of a smile in his voice.

Then the bastard turned the tables and made me tell him everything about Hollie.

And because I was so damn happy that Luke was a part of my life again, I told him everything.

Everything from the day she tried to run me down in the carpark, to the horse riding – at which he raised a very skeptical eyebrow – to the party.

I even told him about kissing her, and the way I treated her afterwards. The words flowed out of me. I hadn't known how cathartic it would be to talk to someone about it all.

And I realised that aside from Hollie, and occasionally, very briefly, Beth, I didn't have anyone to talk to here. I mean … really talk to.

Now, I flop back onto the couch cushions. I have to say, Beth has excellent taste in couches, even if they are a little narrow for sleeping. Luke's still lying flat on his back, hands crossed over his stomach, staring up at that ceiling.

"Do you need anything?" I ask. "Help? Meds? Coffee?"

"What I need is for my body not to hurt constantly," he says quietly. "But coffee and pills will do for now." He shuffles around in the bed a bit, then with a small moan goes still. "And a hand sitting up. Mum warned me that being in a car that long was a terrible idea."

"Yeah, well, you've always been stubborn," I say, reaching over and letting him guide me in helping him sit upright. "I'm sorry it hurts, but I'm glad you came."

"It always hurts, even when I've not travelled," he says with a little grimace. "And I'm glad I came too, mostly because we've got to figure out how to fix the mess you made with that girl."

"Would that girl be Hollie?" Beth asks as she steps into the room, Thea on her hip. I reach out and take the baby from her, grinning as she reaches up to grab at my hair. Luke stares at me as if I'm a completely different person. It's true, in a way. I'm very different to the person to the one he once knew.

I shrug at him. "She's my cousin and we're mates. Right, Thea?" I pause and glance over at Beth, who's watching me closely. I have no idea how much she knows about what's happened between me and Hollie. "Um, yeah, it's Hollie," I say eventually and super awkwardly.

"Look, Johnny," she says. "I don't know what's happened between you two, but I know something happened, okay? I'm not so stupid that I didn't see it when she had dinner here last week. The thing is, you've got a lot of stuff going on, and while she hides it well, Hollie's got a lot of her own stuff going on, especially now. So tread lightly, okay?"

I nod silently.

As dumb as it sounds, it's never really occurred to me that Hollie might have something else going on in her own life that I don't know about. I mean, we've only known each other a couple of weeks – and I haven't told her any of my secrets.

Everything between us has been light, small talk. We've talked about school and the horses and Thea. We briefly covered my family and her friends, but nothing that breached that smooth surface layer – until that night at Dan's party when we talked about my baggage.

She's always seemed so content, so happy, so confident in

who she is. I wonder what she's dealing with. I remember telling her to go back to her perfect life, and wince.

I wonder if I can fix it; if I can redeem myself. Maybe she'll let me in enough to help carry some of her load.

Because I'm beginning to realise that doing things alone is a lot harder than doing it with other people.

"We have a plan," Luke is saying to Beth, launching into the details as I head for the kitchen to make coffee.

"You okay, honey?" Mum asks, entering the kitchen behind me. I didn't see her coming because I was disentangling Thea's fingers from my hair. I've managed to avoid having a one-on-one conversation with Mum so far, but I have to bite the bullet at some point.

"Yeah, I am," I say, setting out mugs. I hold one up for her and she nods. She rests a hand on my shoulder and I lean into her for a second, then she takes the baby from me.

"When are we going home?" I ask, not sure if I want to hear the answer. Ever since she arrived I've been dreading the conversation I have to have with her, when she tells me I'm going back with her to my old life.

Now things are better with Luke, maybe it won't be so bad.

It'll still be hard leaving Beth and Thea.

Even with my head caught up in my own dramas, I still think I've been useful to have around the place. But maybe my dramas have been too much for Beth. She has a lot going on already.

It's also going to hurt leaving Hollie behind, especially if I can somehow repair what we had before that party.

"We? Are you coming with us?" Her eyebrows have crinkled, the way they do when she's confused.

"Isn't that why you're here? To take me home?"

She shakes her head.

"I came to get the car and to visit you. Kris and Luke wanted to see you too. But we weren't going to take you home with us … not unless you want us to."

"Beth isn't kicking me out?" The relief is profound. It's another weight lifted off my chest.

"No, of course not. She's loved having you here. She said you've been settling in, being really helpful on the farm, making some friends. She said you've even been riding."

I nod, still a bit dumbstruck.

"I thought all the crap I've put her through … I thought she was done with me."

"Oh no, Johnny." Mum crosses the room and hugs me. I lean into her, dropping my head to rest it on her shoulder, even though I'm taller than her now. Thea giggles and tugs at my hair. "Sweetie, she said you've been doing better."

"I think I have," I say, "especially now things are better with Luke."

She pats me on the back.

"I don't know what happened between you two, but you both suffered for it. I'm so glad you're talking again."

"Me too. Thanks for bringing him."

"Of course, honey. I'm sorry that things got so hard for you. Dad and I really didn't know how to deal with it. And I'm sorry you felt like you had to come here, that we couldn't help you."

"It wasn't your fault, Mum," I say, finally pulling away. "You did the best you could. I wasn't exactly nice to be around, and I didn't accept any help. But thank you for letting me come here."

She nods. "You let me know if you want to come home

with us tomorrow. It's completely up to you. Beth loves having you here and we'd love to have you home."

I nod and start making the coffee. As I work, I keep talking.

"I'm starting to realise that talking about things, talking to people about what's going on, might be a better option than shutting it all down. I'll work on that, but I wondered if maybe … maybe I needed to see someone about it?"

"Like a counsellor?" She leans against the counter beside the coffee machine, bopping Thea on the nose while the baby giggles and grabs her hand.

"Yeah, maybe," I say, not really sure myself. But it's a thought that's been niggling away at me since last night, when Luke described some of the therapy he's been having post-accident. Mental therapy, he called it, rather than the physical therapy necessary for his body's rehab.

"Of course," she says with a small smile, reaching out to rub my arm. "Anything you think will help."

I smile back and pick up Luke's coffee along with my own and head to the lounge.

Luke is sitting up in the bed and Beth is perched on the edge of the couch, and they're having intense discussions – probably about the likelihood of me getting back into Hollie's good graces.

Luke glances up at me as I make my way towards him.

"Think Johnny has a shot at winning Hollie back?" he asks Beth with a grin.

She studies me a moment. "It's a good idea, but it really depends on Johnny not acting like an idiot, doesn't it?"

Luke mock groans. "So, we've got no hope, then?" He laughs and I roll my eyes at him.

"Shut up," I say, carefully handing him his mug of coffee,

while Mum passes over a container containing various medications and pain killers. "I can at least try."

CHAPTER 33

Hollie

I'M STILL ASLEEP the next morning when there's a light knock on my door.

I pry my eyes open, which takes some effort. They're swollen from yesterday's cry-athon.

I startle when I see Kaitlin's face peering around my bedroom door.

"Hey," she whispers.

"Kait," I say, shocked to see her. I'd completely forgotten about my promise to explain everything to her until two days after the party, by which time she was off on holiday with her family. It didn't help that my phone had been lost for a while after the accident.

When I got it back I texted her over and over, begging her to forgive me, but she didn't reply to any messages.

"Hey," I say, sitting. "Come in."

"You didn't tell me you were in an accident," she scolds. "Are you okay?"

I nod dumbly. "I'm so sorry, Kait. I'm so sorry I didn't come to see you."

"It's okay, you were in a freaking car accident, Holls! I'm sorry I didn't come sooner. I was mad at you at first. I only found out about the crash last night. What happened?"

"But you were at the party. You must have heard."

She shakes her head.

"I left early because I had to get ready and Mum made me promise not to stay out too late. I must have gone right before you did."

"I'm so sorry, Kait. I'm sorry about everything. I don't blame you for being mad at me. I've been a useless friend."

"You haven't," she says, climbing onto my bed beside me. I close my eyes as she wraps an arm around me. I lie in her embrace for a long quiet moment. But it's not an awkward silence.

"I'm sick," I say eventually. "Mentally sick, I mean." And there it is. I've told her. Just like that. "Danny's been the only one who knows, because I've been too scared to tell people. I promise I wasn't lying to you about going out with him."

"I know you weren't," she smirks at me. "Trust me, after seeing you with Jonathan … I'm sorry I ever doubted you. And I'm sorry you felt like you couldn't tell me something like that."

"It's nothing to do with you, Kait." I take a deep breath, steadying myself before continuing. "It scares me so much and it's embarrassing and I feel so stupid. But I'm going to therapy, and maybe I'll start some medication, and maybe Beth will have me back after my leg is better. And I promise I'll be a better friend."

"Babes, you're an excellent friend and definitely not stupid. Whenever you're ready to tell me more, I'm here."

And so I do.

We curl up in my bed, like when we were twelve and

having sleepovers. I tell her about how it affects me, why I got my job, the things I've ticked off my bucket list with Dan and how he's helped me through it all. I explain how at times my brain makes me believe that every interaction I have is negative, even if it really isn't, and how I thought she was always upset with me, for months, because my mind lies to me.

I tell her about giving up riding; that it was because of my depression. Because it got to be too much: the responsibility of having my own horse, the constant pressure I put on myself to compete and do well every time … but that giving up the thing I loved most in the world was actually harder.

She quizzes me on Jonathan and I tell her snippets, trying to avoid the horrible ending. When she pushes I tell her it isn't meant to be, and that while I'm sad, I'm okay about it.

"But why isn't it meant to be? You guys looked really close and *really* into each other at the party." She gives me a cheeky eyebrow waggle and I laugh at her stupid expression.

"Wrong time, maybe? I don't know. Maybe we're not in the right place. I think his mum came yesterday, so maybe he's going home." I try not to let that thought hurt as much as it does.

"You don't want to see him before he goes? See if you can clear some of it up?" She's being gentle with me, but her voice is hopeful, and I realise that yeah, I do want to clear it up. Even if he still hates me.

I need to apologise. Properly.

"Will you come with me?" I ask.

"Of course!" She scrambles off the bed. "Can I do your makeup first?"

I laugh, knowing that everything's okay with Kaitlin again.

Now it's only Jonathan.

"Whatever," I say, and crawl out of bed.

Dan meets us on the doorstep as Kaitlin and I are heading out to her car.

"Oh, hi," he says, probably shocked to see me upright, dressed and with hair and makeup done.

I didn't let Kait go all out – it isn't that kind of occasion – but she's managed to give me a little colour and disguise the dark circles under my eyes.

"Hey, Dan," I say with a small smile. Today feels completely different to yesterday, especially now I've talked things through with Kaitlin.

It turns out she wasn't even mad with me the week before the party. She thought I'd been avoiding her. Maybe I was a little bit, but mostly because I was worried about how mad she was with me. I really have to work on that stupid trick my brain plays on me. I know things are still hard, and one morning of feeling better isn't solving all my problems, but I'll take the little burst of energy I've had this morning.

"Uh," he says. "Are you off somewhere?"

I nod. "I need to talk to him, even if he doesn't want to see me."

"Oh, cool," he says, looking oddly relieved. "Um, mind if I tag along?"

"Not at all," Kait says, linking arms with him while I stumble along on my crutches. "Thanks for looking after her so well," she murmurs to Dan when she thinks she's far enough away.

I smile. I'm pretty lucky with my friends.

We make the drive to Beth's place in happy conversation, Kait telling us about her holiday, and I relax into the seat.

It's the most relaxed – the most calm – I've been for weeks, and I realise that maybe this is how things are going to be, at least for a while. Maybe antidepressants will help, even though I've fought the idea of them all the way along. I've already emailed Dana asking to discuss them at our next appointment, and I'm looking forward to making some progress again, even if it's going to be hard.

Because the good parts of my life outweigh the bad. And it's worth it.

We pull into the driveway just as the dark SUV comes over the hill towards us. I can't make out who's driving, but the vehicle slows then starts reversing back down the driveway, so Kaitlin carries on.

"Maybe this is a bad time. He … he clearly has plans. He's going somewhere," I stumble over the words as the anxiety creeps back in, stealing away my calm.

"He was on his way to see you," Dan says from the backseat.

"What?" I twist to face him. "How do you know that?"

"Because he texted me this morning to ask if I thought you'd ever speak to him again, so he could explain."

"Oh." I fall back into my seat and steady my breath. Maybe this won't be as bad as I thought.

As Kaitlin draws to a stop Jonathan opens my door. "Hey," he says carefully, as I arrange my crutches.

"Hi," I say shyly, awkwardly.

He holds out a hand and I let him pull me up. The warmth in his hand still sends tingles up my arm.

But I'm not here for tingly feelings. I'm here to apologise; to see if we can get past this.

"Look, Hollie," he starts, but I interrupt him.

"I'm really, really sorry, okay? I didn't mean for any of it to happen and I'm really sorry." The words tumble out of my mouth before I can study them for cohesion and sense. "I'll pay for the car, the damage, whatever."

Jonathan stands there, dumbstruck.

"I'm sorry. I shouldn't have taken your car. I'm sorry I pushed you. It was none of my business."

"But—"

"I'm sorry for all of it, and if you want me to stay away I promise I will. I only wanted to apologise first."

"Hollie. Stop."

Words freeze on my tongue. It's probably for the best – I'm not even sure what I've already said.

"You're stealing all my lines."

"Your lines?" I'm so confused.

"I don't even know why you're apologising to me." He says it with a small, sad smile, but it doesn't help me feel any less confused.

"Because I stuck my nose in where you didn't want it, and then I stole your car and crashed it," I reply. Like, what's not to get?

He shakes his head, eyes wide with surprise. "I don't give a crap about my car, Hollie. I care about you."

"You what?"

"I care about you. I care that you're okay, I care that I treated you awfully. I care that you might never speak to me again."

I have no idea what to say. I glance around, wracking my

brain for a response, and notice Beth leading Harley towards us. He's fully saddled. She hands the reins to Jonathan, gives me a quick smile and retreats again.

Harley reaches out and nibbles at my sleeve.

"Hey, boy," I whisper, grateful for the distraction.

"I thought maybe you'd want to go for a ride?" Jonathan says nervously. His hand twitches but doesn't end up tangled in his hair. He twists the reins around his fingers instead.

"Um, I can't ride," I say, gesturing at my leg.

He untangles his fingers and shoves his hand into his hair and I see the flash of a smile. "You know, since you pointed out how often I do that, I notice every time now. And I know you can't ride like you usually do, but if you wanted to, you could ride a little bit."

I study Jonathan, study Harley, think about the logistics of this.

He's right, I can't ride like I usually do – but I *could* ride. At least, I could try.

"Okay," I say with a smile, heading for the mounting block, making slow progress.

Jonathan falls into step beside me, Harley trailing behind.

"Huh," he says and I glance up, following the direction of his gaze.

Dan is helping Luke out of the SUV. When Luke is out Dan's hand stays on his arm for a few moments too long as he looks up into his face.

"Is that … is that what it looks like?" I say.

Jonathan shrugs. "I don't know," he says. "That, by the way, is Luke." He's smiling as he says it – the kind of real smile I've only seen in a photograph up until now.

"I figured." I roll my eyes a little. "I'm not completely dense, you know."

"And," he continues, ignoring my interruption, "we sorted things out. And one day, I'd very much like to explain everything to you."

We've reached the mounting block and I clamber up while Jonathan steers Harley into place. I slide my injured leg over the pony's back and hoist myself on. It's clumsy and awkward and completely unbalanced, but I can do this.

I cross the stirrup over the front of the saddle so it doesn't bang against my cast and settle myself in, taking up the reins. I head for the arena and Jonathan walks beside me, in case I'm going to slide right off, I suppose.

"Hollie, I need to apologise," he says abruptly. "I was a complete and total jerk to you, from the beginning, and I'm really sorry. You've only been nice to me, and I've been awful. I'm sorry for all of it." His voice cracks and I lean over to touch his shoulder, to reassure him that it's okay.

I let out a yelp as I feel the saddle slip from under me. The cast has left me so unbalanced, and that tiny reach has me heading for the ground. I grab for the pommel, hoping I have enough upper body strength to stop myself. I cannot imagine how much it would hurt to land on an already broken leg.

Hands grab my waist and sparks go flying.

Jonathan slides me back into the saddle.

"Holy shit," he says. "Are you okay?"

I take stock, then nod. "I'm fine. Good catch, though."

"I'm sorry. This is such a terrible idea. I'll get Dan to help get you down."

"No." I'm shaking my head before he even finishes speaking. "I'm not done. This wasn't a bad idea. It's actually a great idea."

I reach out and place my hand on his shoulder. He's still standing right up against Harley where he stepped in to catch me. His hands are hovering near my hips and I can feel their warmth.

"I have no idea why you're apologising for so many things. But thank you for this." I gesture at Harley.

"I'm sorry I didn't do it earlier. I thought you hated me, that you blamed me for what happened."

"Why would you think I blamed you?"

"Because it felt like my fault," he says, voice low and rough.

"But you weren't even there," I say, confused as ever about what's going on with him. I thought he was mad at me, but he thought I was mad at him.

"No, but you were only there because of me."

I hadn't thought of it that way. "I never blamed you for any of it," I say eventually. "I thought you were mad at me, for the car, for pushing you too far about Luke."

He sighs and rests his head against Harley's neck. "Ever since I got here, all you've done is be a really good friend to me, but I never felt like I deserved it. Every time I was a jerk I hated myself for it, but I thought it was easier to keep you from getting too close, and being a jerk was the easiest way to do that. Except I couldn't help myself. Being around you was so easy; you made me forget the reasons I thought I didn't deserve you. God, when I kissed you…"

He pushes away from Harley's side and I instantly miss the warmth of him against my leg. He tangles his hands in his hair again then glances up at me, a grin on his face. "Seriously, you have ruined this hair thing for me."

I laugh. "What about when you kissed me?" I ask, breathless and hopeful. Hopeful that I'm going to like where this is going.

"When I kissed you," he says, voice low, "I didn't want to stop." He steps in close again. Harley turns his head to snuffle at Jonathan's pockets. I lean down, wishing I wasn't awkwardly trapped on a horse. "I didn't want to stop," he continues, "but I didn't know how I could get involved with you if I couldn't tell you what happened. I couldn't line up who I was with what I'd done. I needed to explain to you why I was so messed up, but it wasn't my story to tell." He leans into Harley again, rubbing the little horse behind the ears.

"It was Luke's story?" I give his shoulder another squeeze and he nods into the horse's mane.

"Except I didn't realise until yesterday that Luke doesn't remember most of what happened, and the accident was never my fault in the first place – or so he says."

"So, sort of like my accident?" I ask.

"Yeah, so I'm told." He raises his head and finally looks at me again. His face is rueful. "Apparently I have a few things to work on, like not running away from all my problems and not taking the blame for things outside of my control."

"Sounds like a good start," I say. "But you don't have to tell me. Not now, and not ever if you don't want to, or Luke doesn't want you to." I pause. "There are some things I'd like to tell you, too," I whisper, "about what's been going on with me. I'm learning that talking about things helps quite a lot."

"I'd like that." He smiles up at me. "Luke said I can tell you whatever I need to tell you, whatever I need to make things right with you. If any of it will help." He looks nervous again.

"But Jonathan…" I let my words trail off and he gazes up

at me with an unreadable expression on his face. It's some mixture of pain and hope and several other things I can't decipher. "Are you going home? Now that things are better with Luke?"

He takes a deep breath and I shut my eyes, unable to watch him as he answers my question.

His hand brushes against my leg just above the bend in my knee and I draw my own shaking breath. I don't want us to have had this conversation just for him to leave.

"No." His voice is soft and gentle but certain, and I let the word roll over me. I open my eyes, meeting his as his hand settles on my leg. "Beth still needs my help." He gives a little shrug. "And I like being here. It's different to home. I'm not ready to go back yet. I'm not done here." He pauses. "If that's okay with you?"

My breath catches. "Jonathan, can you get me off this horse?" I say. My is voice low but my heart is taking flight.

His soft, hopeful expression flickers and in a blink turns worried. He steps away from me, and I wilt at the loss of his touch.

"I'll get Dan to help." He goes to turn away but I stop him.

"I don't think we need Dan for this," I say, swinging my good leg over the front of the saddle so I'm sitting sideways.

Jonathan's mouth drops open like he wants to speak but doesn't know what to say. He steps in close again though, placing his hands on my waist and firing up those sparks again.

I slide forward and down into his arms. He catches me, cushioning my fall. I land awkwardly on my good leg, giving a little hop, but his arms come around me, a warm band of strength to steady me.

"That better?" His voice is low and husky in my ear, relief evident in his words. His fingers slide into my hair.

"Much," I murmur back, already reaching up to feel his lips against mine.

As they touch, I wrap my arms around his neck and realise my heart is flying and falling, all at the same time.

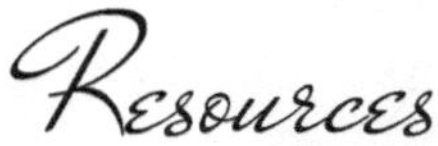

Some of the topics in this book can be confronting.
If you need assistance, please reach out for support.

<u>New Zealand:</u>
Depression Helpline: 0800 111 757 or free text 4202
Youthline: 0800 376 633 or free text 234
The Low Down: Text 5626

<u>Australia:</u>
Beyond Blue: 1300 22 4363
Kids Helpline: 1800 55 1800 (ages 5-25)

<u>United States:</u>
Teen Line: 800 852 8336 or text 839863
Mental` Health America: 1 800 985 5990 or text Talk-WithUs to 66746

<u>United Kingdom:</u>

Give Us A Shout: Text 85258
SANEline: 0300 689 5652

If these numbers don't apply to you, please google your local mental health support line, or reach out to friends, family, or your school.

Acknowledgments

It's hard to believe I'm sitting here writing the acknowledgements for my second book.

I actually wrote this one first, well before *The Stars Burn Bright* was even an idea, and it's had a long and interesting journey. I'm so glad Hollie and Jonathan's story is now getting the chance to go out into the world.

As expected, there are many people who need my thanks.

My husband Chris and my gorgeous daughters, Charlotte, Taylor and Isabelle, are a constant support and light in my life. I know things are not always easy when my head goes to the same place Hollie's does, but you're always there, making it worth it. I love you all so much. (Special thanks to Chris for only mocking me a tiny bit when he came home to find me completely inconsolable about what I'd done to the characters in this book!)

My parents would never buy me books as a child, but always encouraged me to get out there and do things. Plus, they bought me all my horses and traipsed around the country with me so that one day I'd have all the knowledge I needed to write a book about a horse girl. Thanks for that!

I truly have the greatest friends in the world. The friendships in this book are inspired by the amazing, incredible people who've been a part of my life, including (but not limited to): Kelsey and Natalie, Haley, Vanessa and Cathy, Sarah and

Caleb. There are so many more who've been such a light for me, and I can't thank you enough.

Writing a book is kind of a solitary thing, but then it's not, especially when you're a part of the New Zealand author community and #bookstagram. The people I've met and friendships I've formed have made being an author and publisher the best experience. Thank you for your support, encouragement and enthusiasm.

This novel had many early readers because I had no idea what I was doing. Thank you to Haley, Alida, Veronica, Sarah, Yun, Kelsey, Natalie and Alyssa for your encouragement and insight.

Flying and Falling was shortlisted for the Storylines Tessa Duder Award in 2022. Thank you to Storylines for providing such an opportunity (and for the others you've given me since) and to Mandy Hager for her constructive and motivating feedback on my manuscript assessment.

My editing and proofreading was again completed by Patricia Bell. She's such a gem and I hope for her sake that my ability to use a comma improved a little this time around.

Jenn Rackham designed the cover for this book, and just like last time she's done an amazing job capturing the vision inside my head and turning it into a beautiful cover.

Finally, thank you to my readers. Thank you for wanting to read this book. Thank you to everyone who writes a review, shares about it on their social media or recommends it to a friend. I hope you enjoyed the story and want to join me to do it all again (because there is a sort-of sequel…).

Lynda Tomalin lives in a small town in New Zealand, where she writes sweet, swoony books about teenagers finding their place in the world.

She is a mum of three girls and a farmer's wife, and when she's not daydreaming about her fictional characters and trying to find space for all the books she keeps buying, she works in administration (but mostly only to fund making books).

Find her online:
www.lyndatomalinauthor.com
Instagram and Facebook:
@lynda.tomalin.author

Email:
contact@lyndatomalinauthor.com

A sweet, swoon YA romance about discovering and celebrating your worth.

Seventeen-year-old Essie is looking forward to her summer holidays.

It means weeks of dedicating herself to her sewing business while her parents are busy working. Sure, her jerk of a brother is home from university, but he's mostly working too, so it's easy to stay out of his way. She can be herself – whoever she wants to be, without expectation or judgement or always being told she's over-dramatic.

It's going to be amazing.

Until Jackson Sherwood, her brother's childhood friend, comes to stay.

Jax. Essie has no time for the smug jerk who's always smirking at her, like he's so much better than her.

Jax's arrival threatens to ruin her plans for a peaceful summer, but as their situation forces them to spend time together, Essie starts to see a hidden side of the unwanted guest, and starts to learn about herself: who she is, where she fits in the world … and what she's willing to stand up for.